DOVER · THRIFT · EDITIONS

A Midsummer Night's Dream

WILLIAM SHAKESPEARE

DOVER PUBLICATIONS, INC.
New York

DOVER THRIFT EDITIONS

GENERAL EDITOR: STANLEY APPELBAUM
EDITOR OF THIS VOLUME: SHANE WELLER

Performance

This Dover Thrift Edition may be used in its entirety, in adaptation or in any other way for theatrical productions, professional and amateur, in the United States, without fee, permission or acknowledgment. (This may not apply outside of the United States, as copyright conditions may vary.)

Bibliographical Note

This Dover edition, first published in 1992, contains the unabridged text of *A Midsummer Night's Dream* as published in Volume III of *The Caxton Edition of the Complete Works of William Shakespeare*, Caxton Publishing Company, London, n.d. The annotations, which have been prepared specially for the present edition, are based on those given in the third edition of Alexander Schmidt's *Shakespeare-Lexicon*.

Library of Congress Cataloging-in-Publication Data

Shakespeare, William, 1564–1616.
A midsummer night's dream / William Shakespeare.
p.   cm. — (Dover thrift editions)
ISBN-13: 978-0-486-27067-8
ISBN-10: 0-486-27067-X
I. Series.
PR2827.A1   1992
822.3'3—dc20   91-29741
                                                                              CIP

Manufactured in the United States by Courier Corporation
27067X23   2015
www.doverpublications.com

Note

WILLIAM SHAKESPEARE (1564–1616) probably wrote A *Midsummer Night's Dream* between 1594 and 1595. In several respects the play heralds a movement away from the conventionality of the early toward the subtleties and ambiguities of the mature comedies. It demonstrates both Shakespeare's great facility for a wide range of verse forms and rhyme schemes, and his ability to bring together in a single work plots and characters derived from diverse literary sources. The story of the marriage of Theseus, Duke of Athens, and Hippolyta, Queen of the Amazons, was available to Shakespeare in two forms: in Chaucer's *Knight's Tale* and in Thomas North's *Lives of the noble Grecians and Romanes* (1579), a translation of Plutarch. The story of the crossed lovers Lysander, Hermia and Demetrius is also in Chaucer's work, though Shakespeare complicates things by introducing a second woman, Helena, and by playing on the vagaries of love. Bottom and his troupe of Athenian laborers provide an often hilarious depiction of the theatrical world of Elizabethan England. Their play-within-the-play, *Pyramus and Thisbe*, is derived from Arthur Golding's translation of Ovid's *Metamorphoses*. As for Bottom's transformation into an ass, Shakespeare's most likely source was Apuleius' *Golden Ass*, translated by William Adlington in 1566. English folklore and popular literature contained ample material on the "puck," Robin Goodfellow, whereas Oberon and Titania, King and Queen of the Fairies, appear in various literary works, both English and French. Of course, in A *Midsummer Night's Dream* these preexisting literary creations take on a new, inimitably Shakespearean, life.

The play is in part about the potentially tragic conflict between social order and the freedom of the imagination embodied in the young lovers. The experience of love unfolds as a journey away from the city, and the parental and political authority that governs there, into a sylvan realm of fantasy, dream and delusion. Marriage comes to symbolize the reconciliation of forces that in another context would remain in tragic opposition to one another. But, in a typically Shakespearean manner, the play turns upon the metaphor of the theater itself, questioning, sometimes mockingly, sometimes reverently, the nature of art and imagination, and their relationship to the world they reflect and transform.

Contents

Dramatis Personae   ix

Act I   1

Act II   12

Act III   26

Act IV   46

Act V   54

Dramatis Personae

THESEUS, Duke of Athens.
EGEUS, father to Hermia.
LYSANDER, ⎱ in love with Hermia.
DEMETRIUS, ⎰
PHILOSTRATE, master of the revels to Theseus.
QUINCE, a carpenter.
SNUG, a joiner.
BOTTOM, a weaver.
FLUTE, a bellows-mender.
SNOUT, a tinker.
STARVELING, a tailor.

HIPPOLYTA, Queen of the Amazons, betrothed to Theseus.
HERMIA, daughter to Egeus, in love with Lysander.
HELENA, in love with Demetrius.

OBERON, King of the Fairies.
TITANIA, Queen of the Fairies.
PUCK, or Robin Goodfellow.
PEASEBLOSSOM, ⎫
COBWEB, ⎪
MOTH, ⎬ fairies.
MUSTARDSEED, ⎭

Other fairies attending their King and Queen. Attendants on
Theseus and Hippolyta.

SCENE—*Athens, and a wood near it*

A Midsummer
Night's Dream

Act I—Scene I—Athens

THE PALACE OF THESEUS

Enter THESEUS, HIPPOLYTA, PHILOSTRATE, *and* Attendants.

THE.   Now, fair Hippolyta, our nuptial hour
        Draws on apace; four happy days bring in
        Another moon: but, O, methinks, how slow
        This old moon wanes! she lingers[1] my desires,
        Like to a step-dame, or a dowager,
        Long withering out a young man's revenue.

HIP.   Four days will quickly steep themselves in night;
        Four nights will quickly dream away the time;
        And then the moon, like to a silver bow
        New-bent in heaven, shall behold the night
        Of our solemnities.[2]

THE.   Go, Philostrate,
        Stir up the Athenian youth to merriments;
        Awake the pert[3] and nimble spirit of mirth:
        Turn melancholy forth to funerals;
        The pale companion is not for our pomp. [*Exit* PHILOSTRATE.
        Hippolyta, I woo'd thee with my sword,
        And won thy love, doing thee injuries;
        But I will wed thee in another key,
        With pomp, with triumph[4] and with revelling.

Enter EGEUS, HERMIA, LYSANDER, *and* DEMETRIUS.

---

[1] *lingers*] prolongs.
[2] *solemnities*] celebration (of the wedding).
[3] *pert*] lively.
[4] *triumph*] public festivity.

1

EGE. Happy be Theseus, our renowned duke!
THE. Thanks, good Egeus: what's the news with thee?
EGE. Full of vexation come I, with complaint
      Against my child, my daughter Hermia.
      Stand forth, Demetrius. My noble lord,
      This man hath my consent to marry her.
      Stand forth, Lysander: and, my gracious duke,
      This man hath bewitch'd the bosom[5] of my child:
      Thou, thou, Lysander, thou hast given her rhymes,
      And interchanged love-tokens with my child:
      Thou hast by moonlight at her window sung,
      With feigning[6] voice, verses of feigning love;
      And stolen the impression of her fantasy[7]
      With bracelets of thy hair, rings, gawds, conceits,[8]
      Knacks,[9] trifles, nosegays, sweetmeats, messengers
      Of strong prevailment[10] in unharden'd[11] youth:
      With cunning hast thou filch'd my daughter's heart;
      Turn'd her obedience, which is due to me,
      To stubborn harshness: and, my gracious duke,
      Be it so she will not here before your Grace
      Consent to marry with Demetrius,
      I beg the ancient privilege of Athens,
      As she is mine, I may dispose of her:
      Which shall be either to this gentleman
      Or to her death, according to our law
      Immediately[12] provided in that case.
THE. What say you, Hermia? be advised, fair maid:
      To you your father should be as a god;
      One that composed your beauties; yea, and one
      To whom you are but as a form in wax
      By him imprinted and within his power
      To leave the figure or disfigure it.
      Demetrius is a worthy gentleman.
HER. So is Lysander.

      [5] *bosom*] heart.
      [6] *feigning*] soft.
      [7] *stolen . . . fantasy*] captured her imagination and love.
      [8] *gawds, conceits*] baubles, fanciful presents.
      [9] *Knacks*] knickknacks.
      [10] *prevailment*] influence.
      [11] *unharden'd*] impressionable.
      [12] *Immediately*] expressly.

THE.   In himself he is;
          But in this kind, wanting your father's voice,[13]
          The other must be held the worthier.
HER.   I would my father look'd but with my eyes.
THE.   Rather your eyes must with his judgement look.
HER.   I do entreat your Grace to pardon me.
          I know not by what power I am made bold,
          Nor how it may concern[14] my modesty,
          In such a presence here to plead my thoughts;
          But I beseech your Grace that I may know
          The worst that may befall me in this case,
          If I refuse to wed Demetrius.
THE.   Either to die the death, or to abjure
          For ever the society of men.
          Therefore, fair Hermia, question your desires;
          Know of your youth, examine well your blood,
          Whether, if you yield not to your father's choice,
          You can endure the livery of a nun;
          For aye[15] to be in shady cloister mew'd,[16]
          To live a barren sister all your life,
          Chanting faint hymns to the cold fruitless moon.
          Thrice-blessed they that master so their blood,
          To undergo such maiden pilgrimage;
          But earthlier happy is the rose distill'd,[17]
          Than that which, withering on the virgin thorn,
          Grows, lives, and dies in single blessedness.
HER.   So will I grow, so live, so die, my lord,
          Ere I will yield my virgin patent[18] up
          Unto his lordship, whose unwished yoke
          My soul consents not to give sovereignty.
THE.   Take time to pause; and, by the next new moon,—
          The sealing-day betwixt my love and me,
          For everlasting bond of fellowship,—
          Upon that day either prepare to die
          For disobedience to your father's will,

[13] *in this kind . . . voice*] in business of this nature, lacking your father's approval.
[14] *concern*] befit.
[15] *aye*] ever.
[16] *mew'd*] confined.
[17] *earthlier . . . distill'd*] i.e., happier on earth is the one who will live on after death through his or her child.
[18] *virgin patent*] privilege of remaining a virgin.

               Or else to wed Demetrius, as he would;
               Or on Diana's altar to protest[19]
               For aye austerity and single life.

DEM.   Relent, sweet Hermia: and, Lysander, yield
               Thy crazed title[20] to my certain right.

LYS.   You have her father's love, Demetrius;
               Let me have Hermia's: do you marry him.

EGE.   Scornful Lysander! true, he hath my love,
               And what is mine my love shall render him.
               And she is mine, and all my right of her
               I do estate unto Demetrius.

LYS.   I am, my lord, as well derived[21] as he,
               As well possess'd;[22] my love is more than his;
               My fortunes every way as fairly rank'd,
               If not with vantage,[23] as Demetrius';
               And, which is more than all these boasts can be,
               I am beloved of beauteous Hermia:
               Why should not I then prosecute my right?
               Demetrius, I'll avouch it to his head,[24]
               Made love to Nedar's daughter, Helena,
               And won her soul; and she, sweet lady, dotes,
               Devoutly dotes, dotes in idolatry,
               Upon this spotted[25] and inconstant man.

THE.   I must confess that I have heard so much,
               And with Demetrius thought to have spoke thereof;
               But, being over-full of self-affairs,
               My mind did lose it. But, Demetrius, come;
               And come, Egeus; you shall go with me,
               I have some private schooling[26] for you both.
               For you, fair Hermia, look you arm yourself
               To fit your fancies[27] to your father's will;
               Or else the law of Athens yields you up, —
               Which by no means we may extenuate, —[28]

[19] *protest*] vow.
[20] *crazed title*] invalid claim.
[21] *well derived*] nobly born.
[22] *well possess'd*] wealthy.
[23] *vantage*] superiority.
[24] *avouch it to his head*] declare it in his presence.
[25] *spotted*] guilty.
[26] *schooling*] admonition.
[27] *fancies*] thoughts of love.
[28] *extenuate*] mitigate.

  To death, or to a vow of single life.
  Come, my Hippolyta: what cheer, my love?
  Demetrius and Egeus, go along:
  I must employ you in some business
  Against[29] our nuptial, and confer with you
  Of something nearly that concerns yourselves.
EGE. With duty and desire we follow you.
        [Exeunt all but LYSANDER *and* HERMIA.
LYS. How now, my love! why is your cheek so pale?
  How chance the roses there do fade so fast?
HER. Belike for want of rain, which I could well
  Beteem[30] them from the tempest of my eyes.
LYS. Ay me! for aught that I could ever read,
  Could ever hear by tale or history,
  The course of true love never did run smooth;
  But, either it was different in blood,—
HER. O cross![31] too high to be enthrall'd to low.
LYS. Or else misgraffed in respect of years,—
HER. O spite! too old to be engaged to young.
LYS. Or else it stood upon the choice of friends,—
HER. O hell! to choose love by another's eyes.
LYS. Or, if there were a sympathy in choice,
  War, death, or sickness did lay siege to it,
  Making it momentany as a sound,
  Swift as a shadow, short as any dream;
  Brief as the lightning in the collied[32] night,
  That, in a spleen,[33] unfolds both heaven and earth,
  And ere a man hath power to say "Behold!"
  The jaws of darkness do devour it up:
  So quick bright things come to confusion.[34]
HER. If then true lovers have been ever cross'd,[35]
  It stands as an edict in destiny:
  Then let us teach our trial patience,
  Because it is a customary cross,

---

[29] *against*] in preparation for.
[30] *Beteem*] grant.
[31] *cross*] The cross symbolizes here that which thwarts or hinders.
[32] *collied*] dark.
[33] *spleen*] fit of passion.
[34] *confusion*] ruin.
[35] *ever cross'd*] always thwarted.

As due to love as thoughts and dreams and sighs,
Wishes and tears, poor fancy's followers.

LYS.   A good persuasion:[36] therefore, hear me, Hermia.
I have a widow aunt, a dowager
Of great revenue, and she hath no child:
From Athens is her house remote seven leagues;
And she respects me as[37] her only son.
There, gentle Hermia, may I marry thee;
And to that place the sharp Athenian law
Cannot pursue us. If thou lovest me, then,
Steal forth thy father's house to-morrow night;
And in the wood, a league without the town,
Where I did meet thee once with Helena,
To do observance to a morn of May,[38]
There will I stay for thee.

HER.   My good Lysander!
I swear to thee, by Cupid's strongest bow,
By his best arrow with the golden head,
By the simplicity of Venus' doves,
By that which knitteth souls and prospers loves,
And by that fire which burn'd the Carthage queen,
When the false Troyan[39] under sail was seen,
By all the vows that ever men have broke,
In number more than ever women spoke,
In that same place thou hast appointed me,
To-morrow truly will I meet with thee.

LYS.   Keep promise, love. Look, here comes Helena.

Enter HELENA.

HER.   God speed fair Helena! whither away?
HEL.   Call you me fair? that fair again unsay.
Demetrius loves your fair: O happy fair!
Your eyes are lode-stars;[40] and your tongue's sweet air
More tuneable[41] than lark to shepherd's ear,
When wheat is green, when hawthorn buds appear.
Sickness is catching: O, were favour so,

[36] *persuasion*] opinion.
[37] *respects me as*] thinks of me as.
[38] *do observance to a morn of May*] celebrate May Day.
[39] *false Troyan*] Aeneas, who abandoned his lover Dido, Queen of Carthage.
[40] *lode-stars*] stars that guide and attract.
[41] *tuneable*] harmonious.

Yours would I catch, fair Hermia, ere I go;
My ear should catch your voice, my eye your eye,
My tongue should catch your tongue's sweet melody.
Were the world mine, Demetrius being bated,[42]
The rest I'd give to be to you translated.[43]
O, teach me how you look; and with what art
You sway the motion[44] of Demetrius' heart!

HER.   I frown upon him, yet he loves me still.
HEL.   O that your frowns would teach my smiles such skill!
HER.   I give him curses, yet he gives me love.
HEL.   O that my prayers could such affection move![45]
HER.   The more I hate, the more he follows me.
HEL.   The more I love, the more he hateth me.
HER.   His folly, Helena, is no fault of mine.
HEL.   None, but your beauty: would that fault were mine!
HER.   Take comfort: he no more shall see my face;
Lysander and myself will fly this place.
Before the time I did Lysander see,
Seem'd Athens as a paradise to me:
O, then, what graces in my love do dwell,
That he hath turn'd a heaven unto a hell!

LYS.   Helen, to you our minds we will unfold:
To-morrow night, when Phoebe[46] doth behold
Her silver visage in the watery glass,[47]
Decking with liquid pearl the bladed grass,
A time that lovers' flights doth still conceal,
Through Athens' gates have we devised to steal.

HER.   And in the wood, where often you and I
Upon faint[48] primrose-beds were wont to lie,
Emptying our bosoms of their counsel sweet,
There my Lysander and myself shall meet;
And thence from Athens turn away our eyes,
To seek new friends and stranger companies.
Farewell, sweet playfellow: pray thou for us;
And good luck grant thee thy Demetrius!

[42] *bated*] excepted.
[43] *to you translated*] transformed into you.
[44] *sway the motion*] control the impulse.
[45] *such affection move*] arouse such passion.
[46] *Phoebe*] the goddess of the moon.
[47] *glass*] mirror.
[48] *faint*] pale.

    Keep word, Lysander: we must starve our sight
    From lovers' food till morrow deep midnight.
LYS. I will, my Hermia.   [*Exit* HERMIA.
      Helena, adieu:
    As you on him, Demetrius dote on you!   [*Exit.*
HEL. How happy some o'er other some can be!
    Through Athens I am thought as fair as she.
    But what of that? Demetrius thinks not so;
    He will not know what all but he do know:
    And as he errs, doting on Hermia's eyes,
    So I, admiring of his qualities:
    Things base and vile, holding no quantity,[49]
    Love can transpose to form and dignity:
    Love looks not with the eyes, but with the mind;
    And therefore is wing'd Cupid painted blind:
    Nor hath Love's mind of any judgement taste;
    Wings, and no eyes, figure[50] unheedy haste:
    And therefore is Love said to be a child,
    Because in choice he is so oft beguiled.
    As waggish boys in game themselves forswear,
    So the boy Love is perjured everywhere:
    For ere Demetrius look'd on Hermia's eyne,[51]
    He hail'd down oaths that he was only mine;
    And when this hail some heat from Hermia felt,
    So he dissolved, and showers of oaths did melt.
    I will go tell him of fair Hermia's flight:
    Then to the wood will he to-morrow night
    Pursue her; and for this intelligence
    If I have thanks, it is a dear expense:
    But herein mean I to enrich my pain,
    To have his sight thither and back again.   [*Exit.*

[49] *holding no quantity*] not having the value given them.
[50] *figure*] symbolize.
[51] *eyne*] eyes.

Scene II—The same

QUINCE'S HOUSE

Enter QUINCE, SNUG, BOTTOM, FLUTE, SNOUT, *and* STARVELING.

QUIN. Is all our company here?

BOT. You were best to call them generally,[1] man by man, according to the scrip.[2]

QUIN. Here is the scroll of every man's name, which is thought fit, through all Athens, to play in our interlude[3] before the duke and the duchess, on his wedding-day at night.

BOT. First, good Peter Quince, say what the play treats on; then read the names of the actors; and so grow to a point.[4]

QUIN. Marry, our play is, The most lamentable comedy, and most cruel death of Pyramus and Thisbe.

BOT. A very good piece of work, I assure you, and a merry. Now, good Peter Quince, call forth your actors by the scroll. Masters, spread yourselves.

QUIN. Answer as I call you. Nick Bottom, the weaver.

BOT. Ready. Name what part I am for, and proceed.

QUIN. You, Nick Bottom, are set down for Pyramus.

BOT. What is Pyramus? a lover, or a tyrant?

QUIN. A lover, that kills himself most gallant for love.

BOT. That will ask some tears in the true performing of it: if I do it, let the audience look to their eyes; I will move storms, I will condole[5] in some measure. To the rest: yet my chief humour[6] is for a tyrant: I could play Ercles[7] rarely, or a part to tear a cat in, to make all split.[8]

> The raging rocks
> And shivering shocks
> Shall break the locks
> Of prison-gates;

[1] *generally*] Bottom's malapropism for "severally" (one by one).
[2] *scrip*] written list.
[3] *interlude*] short play.
[4] *grow to a point*] get to the end.
[5] *condole*] show signs of lamentation.
[6] *humour*] inclination.
[7] *Ercles*] Hercules.
[8] *a part . . . split*] a dramatic role that allows for ranting and extravagant gestures.

> And Phibbus' car[9]
> Shall shine from far,
> And make and mar
>   The foolish Fates.

This was lofty! Now name the rest of the players. This is Ercles' vein,
a tyrant's vein; a lover is more condoling.

QUIN. Francis Flute, the bellows-mender.

FLU. Here, Peter Quince.

QUIN. Flute, you must take Thisbe on you.

FLU. What is Thisbe? a wandering knight?[10]

QUIN. It is the lady that Pyramus must love.

FLU. Nay, faith, let not me play a woman; I have a beard coming.

QUIN. That's all one: you shall play it in a mask, and you may speak as
small[11] as you will.

BOT. An[12] I may hide my face, let me play Thisbe too, I'll speak in a
monstrous little voice, "Thisne, Thisne;" "Ah Pyramus, my lover
dear! thy Thisbe dear, and lady dear!"

QUIN. No, no; you must play Pyramus: and, Flute, you Thisbe.

BOT. Well, proceed.

QUIN. Robin Starveling, the tailor.

STAR. Here, Peter Quince.

QUIN. Robin Starveling, you must play Thisbe's mother. Tom Snout,
the tinker.

SNOUT. Here, Peter Quince.

QUIN. You, Pyramus' father: myself, Thisbe's father: Snug, the joiner;
you, the lion's part: and, I hope, here is a play fitted.

SNUG. Have you the lion's part written? pray you, if it be, give it me, for I
am slow of study.

QUIN. You may do it extempore, for it is nothing but roaring.

BOT. Let me play the lion too: I will roar, that I will do any man's heart
good to hear me; I will roar, that I will make the duke say, "Let him
roar again, let him roar again."

QUIN. An you should do it too terribly, you would fright the duchess and
the ladies, that they would shriek; and that were enough to hang us
all.

ALL. That would hang us, every mother's son.

---

[9] *Phibbus' car*] Phoebus Apollo's chariot, the sun.
[10] *wandering knight*] knight-errant.
[11] *as small*] in as clear and high-pitched a voice.
[12] *An*] if.

BOT.   I grant you, friends, if you should fright the ladies out of their wits, they would have no more discretion but to hang us: but I will aggravate[13] my voice so, that I will roar you as gently as any sucking dove; I will roar you an't were any nightingale.

QUIN.   You can play no part but Pyramus; for Pyramus is a sweet-faced man; a proper[14] man, as one shall see in a summer's day; a most lovely, gentleman-like man: therefore you must needs play Pyramus.

BOT.   Well, I will undertake it. What beard were I best to play it in?

QUIN.   Why, what you will.

BOT.   I will discharge[15] it in either your straw colour beard, your orange-tawny beard, your purple-in-grain[16] beard, or your French crown[17] colour beard, your perfect yellow.

QUIN.   Some of your French crowns[18] have no hair at all, and then you will play barefaced. But, masters, here are your parts: and I am to entreat you, request you, and desire you, to con[19] them by tomorrow night; and meet me in the palace wood, a' mile without the town, by moonlight; there will we rehearse, for if we meet in the city, we shall be dogged with company, and our devices known. In the mean time I will draw a bill of properties, such as our play wants. I pray you, fail me not.

BOT.   We will meet; and there we may rehearse most obscenely[20] and courageously. Take pains; be perfect:[21] adieu.

QUIN.   At the duke's oak we meet.

BOT.   Enough; hold or cut bow-strings.[22]

[Exeunt.

---

[13] *aggravate*] Bottom's malapropism for "diminish" (tone down).

[14] *proper*] handsome.

[15] *discharge*] perform.

[16] *purple-in-grain*] scarlet or crimson.

[17] *crown*] coin.

[18] *crowns*] heads, bald as a result of syphilis.

[19] *con*] memorize.

[20] *obscenely*] Bottom's error for "seemly."

[21] *perfect*] word-perfect.

[22] *hold . . . bow-strings*] i.e., be there or give up the play altogether.

Act II—Scene I—A wood near Athens

Enter, from opposite sides, a FAIRY *and* PUCK.

PUCK. How now, spirit! whither wander you?
FAI.   Over hill, over dale,
     Thorough[1] bush, thorough brier,
   Over park, over pale,
     Thorough flood, thorough fire,
   I do wander every where,
   Swifter than the moon's sphere;
   And I serve the fairy queen,
   To dew her orbs upon the green.[2]
   The cowslips tall her pensioners[3] be:
   In their gold coats spots you see;
   Those be rubies, fairy favours,
   In those freckles live their savours:[4]
   I must go seek some dewdrops here,
   And hang a pearl in every cowslip's ear.
   Farewell, thou lob of[5] spirits; I'll be gone:
   Our queen and all her elves come here anon.
PUCK. The king doth keep his revels here to-night:
   Take heed the queen come not within his sight;
   For Oberon is passing fell and wrath,[6]
   Because that she as her attendant hath

---

[1] *Thorough*] through.
[2] *To dew her orbs upon the green*] to sprinkle with dew the fairy rings on the village green.
[3] *pensioners*] bodyguards.
[4] *their savours*] the cowslips' fragrance.
[5] *lob of*] country bumpkin among.
[6] *passing fell and wrath*] exceedingly fierce and angry.

A lovely boy, stolen from an Indian king;
She never had so sweet a changeling:[7]
And jealous Oberon would have the child
Knight of his train, to trace[8] the forests wild;
But she perforce[9] withholds the loved boy,
Crowns him with flowers, and makes him all her joy:
And now they never meet in grove or green,
By fountain clear, or spangled starlight sheen,
But they do square,[10] that all their elves for fear
Creep into acorn cups and hide them there.

FAI.   Either I mistake your shape and making quite,
Or else you are that shrewd[11] and knavish sprite
Call'd Robin Goodfellow:[12] are not you he
That frights the maidens of the villagery;
Skim milk, and sometimes labour in the quern,[13]
And bootless[14] make the breathless housewife churn;
And sometime make the drink to bear no barm;[15]
Mislead night-wanderers, laughing at their harm?
Those that Hobgoblin call you, and sweet Puck,
You do their work, and they shall have good luck:
Are not you he?

PUCK.   Thou speak'st aright;
I am that merry wanderer of the night.
I jest to Oberon, and make him smile,
When I a fat and bean-fed horse beguile,
Neighing in likeness of a filly foal:
And sometimes lurk I in a gossip's bowl,[16]
In very likeness of a roasted crab;[17]
And when she drinks, against her lips I bob
And on her withered dewlap[18] pour the ale.

---

[7] *changeling*] "Changeling" is normally the name for the frail fairy child left in place of
a stolen child. In this instance, however, the changeling is the stolen child.

[8] *trace*] range.

[9] *perforce*] by means of force.

[10] *square*] quarrel.

[11] *shrewd*] mischievous.

[12] *Robin Goodfellow*] a mischievous sprite in English folklore.

[13] *quern*] hand mill for grinding grain.

[14] *bootless*] in vain.

[15] *barm*] yeast or froth.

[16] *a gossip's bowl*] a gossiping old woman's drink of spiced ale with crab apples.

[17] *crab*] crab apple.

[18] *dewlap*] wrinkled skin on the neck.

The wisest aunt,[19] telling the saddest tale,
Sometime for three-foot stool mistaketh me;
Then slip I from her bum, down topples she,
And "tailor" cries, and falls into a cough;
And then the whole quire[20] hold their hips and laugh;
And waxen in their mirth, and neeze,[21] and swear
A merrier hour was never wasted there.
But, room, fairy! here comes Oberon.

FAI. And here my mistress. Would that he were gone!

Enter, from one side, OBERON, *with his train; from the other,* TITANIA, *with hers.*

OBE. Ill met by moonlight, proud Titania.

TITA. What, jealous Oberon! Fairies, skip hence:
I have forsworn his bed and company.

OBE. Tarry, rash wanton: am not I thy lord?

TITA. Then I must be thy lady: but I know
When thou hast stolen away from fairy land,
And in the shape of Corin sat all day,
Playing on pipes of corn, and versing love
To amorous Phillida.[22] Why art thou here,
Come from the farthest steep of India?
But that, forsooth, the bouncing Amazon,
Your buskin'd[23] mistress and your warrior love,
To Theseus must be wedded, and you come
To give their bed joy and prosperity.

OBE. How canst thou thus for shame, Titania,
Glance at[24] my credit with Hippolyta,
Knowing I know thy love to Theseus?
Didst thou not lead him through the glimmering night
From Perigenia, whom he ravished?
And make him with fair Aegle break his faith,
With Ariadne and Antiopa?

TITA. These are the forgeries of jealousy:
And never, since the middle summer's spring,[25]

---

[19] *aunt*] old gossip.
[20] *quire*] company.
[21] *neeze*] sneeze.
[22] *Corin . . . Phillida*] traditional names for pastoral lovers.
[23] *buskin'd*] wearing buskins (laced boots reaching halfway to the knee).
[24] *Glance at*] hint at, censure.
[25] *middle summer's spring*] beginning of midsummer.

Met we on hill, in dale, forest, or mead,
By paved fountain or by rushy brook,
Or in[26] the beached margent[27] of the sea,
To dance our ringlets[28] to the whistling wind,
But with thy brawls thou hast disturb'd our sport.
Therefore the winds, piping to us in vain,
As in revenge, have suck'd up from the sea
Contagious fogs; which, falling in the land,
Have every pelting[29] river made so proud,
That they have overborne their continents:[30]
The ox hath therefore stretch'd his yoke in vain,
The ploughman lost his sweat; and the green corn
Hath rotted ere his youth attain'd a beard:
The fold stands empty in the drowned field,
And crows are fatted with the murrion[31] flock;
The nine men's morris[32] is fill'd up with mud;
And the quaint mazes in the wanton green,[33]
For lack of tread, are undistinguishable:
The human mortals want their winter here;[34]
No night is now with hymn or carol blest:
Therefore the moon, the governess of floods,
Pale in her anger, washes all the air,
That rheumatic diseases do abound:
And thorough this distemperature we see
The seasons alter: hoary-headed frosts
Fall in the fresh lap of the crimson rose;
And on old Hiems'[35] thin and icy crown
An odorous chaplet[36] of sweet summer buds
Is, as in mockery, set: the spring, the summer,
The childing[37] autumn, angry winter, change

[26] *in*] on.
[27] *margent*] edge.
[28] *ringlets*] circular dances.
[29] *pelting*] paltry.
[30] *continents*] banks.
[31] *murrion*] diseased.
[32] *nine men's morris*] a game played with nine counters on the village green.
[33] *quaint mazes in the wanton green*] labyrinthine figures made on the lush village green.
[34] *want . . . here*] lack their usual winter mood.
[35] *Hiems'*] Hiems is the personification of winter.
[36] *chaplet*] garland.
[37] *childing*] fruitful.

Their wonted liveries; and the mazed[38] world,
By their increase, now knows not which is which:
And this same progeny of evils comes
From our debate, from our dissension;
We are their parents and original.[39]

OBE.   Do you amend it, then; it lies in you:
Why should Titania cross her Oberon?
I do but beg a little changeling boy,
To be my henchman.[40]

TITA.   Set your heart at rest:
The fairy land buys not the child of me.
His mother was a votaress of my order:
And, in the spiced Indian air, by night,
Full often hath she gossip'd by my side;
And sat with me on Neptune's yellow sands,
Marking the embarked traders on the flood;
When we have laugh'd to see the sails conceive
And grow big-bellied with the wanton wind;
Which she, with pretty and with swimming gait[41]
Following,—her womb then rich with my young squire,—
Would imitate, and sail upon the land,
To fetch me trifles, and return again,
As from a voyage, rich with merchandise.
But she, being mortal, of that boy did die;
And for her sake do I rear up her boy;
And for her sake I will not part with him.

OBE.   How long within this wood intend you stay?
TITA.   Perchance till after Theseus' wedding-day.
If you will patiently dance in our round,
And see our moonlight revels, go with us;
If not, shun me, and I will spare your haunts.

OBE.   Give me that boy, and I will go with thee.
TITA.   Not for thy fairy kingdom. Fairies, away!
We shall chide downright, if I longer stay.

                                        [*Exit* TITANIA *with her train.*

OBE.   Well, go thy way: thou shalt not from this grove
Till I torment thee for this injury.

---

[38] *mazed*] perplexed.
[39] *original*] source.
[40] *henchman*] page boy.
[41] *swimming gait*] gliding step.

My gentle Puck, come hither. Thou rememberest
Since once I sat upon a promontory,
And heard a mermaid, on a dolphin's back,
Uttering such dulcet and harmonious breath,[42]
That the rude sea grew civil at her song,
And certain stars shot madly from their spheres,
To hear the sea-maid's music.

PUCK.   I remember.

OBE.   That very time I saw, but thou couldst not,
Flying between the cold moon and the earth,
Cupid all arm'd: a certain aim he took
At a fair vestal throned by the west,
And loosed his love-shaft smartly from his bow,
As it should pierce a hundred thousand hearts:
But I might see young Cupid's fiery shaft
Quench'd in the chaste beams of the watery moon,
And the imperial votaress passed on,
In maiden meditation, fancy-free.[43]
Yet mark'd I where the bolt of Cupid fell:
It fell upon a little western flower,
Before milk-white, now purple with love's wound,
And maidens call it love-in-idleness.[44]
Fetch me that flower; the herb I shew'd thee once:
The juice of it on sleeping eye-lids laid
Will make or man or woman madly dote
Upon the next live creature that it sees.
Fetch me this herb; and be thou here again
Ere the leviathan[45] can swim a league.

PUCK.   I'll put a girdle round about the earth
In forty minutes.   [Exit.

OBE.   Having once this juice,
I'll watch Titania when she is asleep,
And drop the liquor of it in her eyes.
The next thing then she waking looks upon,
Be it on lion, bear, or wolf, or bull,
On meddling monkey, or on busy ape,
She shall pursue it with the soul of love:

[42] *breath*] notes, words.
[43] *fancy-free*] free from love.
[44] *love-in-idleness*] a popular name for the pansy.
[45] *leviathan*] sea monster.

And ere I take this charm from off her sight,
As I can take it with another herb,
I'll make her render up her page to me.
But who comes here? I am invisible;
And I will overhear their conference.

Enter DEMETRIUS, HELENA *following him.*

DEM.   I love thee not, therefore pursue me not.
Where is Lysander and fair Hermia?
The one I'll slay, the other slayeth me.
Thou told'st me they were stolen unto this wood;
And here am I, and wode[46] within this wood;
Because I cannot meet my Hermia.
Hence, get thee gone, and follow me no more.

HEL.   You draw me, you hard-hearted adamant;[47]
But yet you draw not iron, for my heart
Is true as steel: leave you[48] your power to draw,
And I shall have no power to follow you.

DEM.   Do I entice you? do I speak you fair?[49]
Or, rather, do I not in plainest truth
Tell you, I do not nor I cannot love you?

HEL.   And even for that do I love you the more.
I am your spaniel; and, Demetrius,
The more you beat me, I will fawn on you:
Use me but as your spaniel, spurn me, strike me,
Neglect me, lose me; only give me leave,
Unworthy as I am, to follow you.
What worser place can I beg in your love,—
And yet a place of high respect with me,—
Than to be used as you use your dog?

DEM.   Tempt not too much the hatred of my spirit;
For I am sick when I do look on thee.

HEL.   And I am sick when I look not on you.

DEM.   You do impeach your modesty too much,
To leave the city, and commit yourself
Into the hands of one that loves you not;
To trust the opportunity of night

---

[46] *wode*] mad, frantic. The normal Shakespearean form of "wode" is "wood."
[47] *adamant*] lodestone.
[48] *leave you*] abandon.
[49] *fair*] kindly.

And the ill counsel of a desert place
With the rich worth of your virginity.
HEL.   Your virtue is my privilege:[50] for that[51]
It is not night when I do see your face,
Therefore I think I am not in the night;
Nor doth this wood lack worlds of company,
For you in my respect[52] are all the world:
Then how can it be said I am alone,
When all the world is here to look on me?
DEM.   I'll run from thee and hide me in the brakes,[53]
And leave thee to the mercy of wild beasts.
HEL.   The wildest hath not such a heart as you.
Run when you will, the story shall be changed:
Apollo flies, and Daphne holds the chase;[54]
The dove pursues the griffin;[55] the mild hind
Makes speed to catch the tiger; bootless speed,
When cowardice pursues, and valour flies.
DEM.   I will not stay thy questions;[56] let me go:
Or, if thou follow me, do not believe
But I shall do thee mischief in the wood.
HEL.   Ay, in the temple, in the town, the field,
You do me mischief. Fie, Demetrius!
Your wrongs do set a scandal on my sex:
We cannot fight for love, as men may do;
We should be woo'd, and were not made to woo. *[Exit* DEM.
I'll follow thee, and make a heaven of hell,
To die upon[57] the hand I love so well.   *[Exit.*
OBE.   Fare thee well, nymph: ere he do leave this grove,
Thou shalt fly him, and he shall seek thy love.

Re-enter PUCK.

Hast thou the flower there? Welcome, wanderer.
PUCK.   Ay, there it is.

---

[50] *privilege]* safeguard:
[51] *for that]* since.
[52] *in my respect]* in my opinion.
[53] *brakes]* thickets.
[54] *Apollo . . . chase]* an allusion to the myth in which the amorous god Apollo pursues Daphne.
[55] *griffin]* a mythical beast with the head of an eagle and the body of a lion.
[56] *stay thy questions]* wait around for your arguments.
[57] *upon]* by.

OBE.   I pray thee, give it me.
　　　　I know a bank where the wild thyme blows,
　　　　Where oxlips and the nodding violet grows;
　　　　Quite over-canopied with luscious woodbine,
　　　　With sweet musk-roses, and with eglantine:
　　　　There sleeps Titania sometime of the night,
　　　　Lull'd in these flowers with dances and delight;
　　　　And there the snake throws her enamell'd skin,
　　　　Weed[58] wide enough to wrap a fairy in:
　　　　And with the juice of this I'll streak[59] her eyes,
　　　　And make her full of hateful fantasies.
　　　　Take thou some of it, and seek through this grove:
　　　　A sweet Athenian lady is in love
　　　　With a disdainful youth: anoint his eyes;
　　　　But do it when the next thing he espies
　　　　May be the lady: thou shalt know the man
　　　　By the Athenian garments he hath on.
　　　　Effect it with some care that he may prove
　　　　More fond on her than she upon her love:
　　　　And look thou meet me ere the first cock crow.
PUCK. Fear not, my lord, your servant shall do so.   [*Exeunt.*

Scene II—Another part of the wood

Enter TITANIA, *with her train.*

TITA.   Come, now a roundel[1] and a fairy song;
　　　　Then, for the third part of a minute, hence;
　　　　Some to kill cankers[2] in the musk-rose buds;
　　　　Some war with rere-mice[3] for their leathern wings,
　　　　To make my small elves coats; and some keep back
　　　　The clamorous owl, that nightly hoots and wonders
　　　　At our quaint spirits. Sing me now asleep;
　　　　Then to your offices, and let me rest.

[58] *Weed*] garment.
[59] *streak*] anoint.

[1] *roundel*] dance in a circle.
[2] *cankers*] caterpillars.
[3] *rere-mice*] bats.

Song

FIRST FAI.   You spotted snakes with double tongue,
        Thorny hedgehogs, be not seen;
    Newts[4] and blind-worms, do no wrong,
        Come not near our fairy queen.

Chorus

    Philomel,[5] with melody
    Sing in our sweet lullaby;
Lulla, lulla, lullaby, lulla, lulla, lullaby:
     Never harm,
     Nor spell, nor charm,
    Come our lovely lady nigh;
    So, good night, with lullaby.

FIRST FAI.   Weaving spiders, come not here;
        Hence, you long-legg'd spinners, hence!
Beetles black, approach not near;
        Worm nor snail, do no offence.

Chorus

    Philomel, with melody, &c.

SEC. FAI.   Hence, away! now all is well:
      One aloof stand sentinel.   [*Exeunt* Fairies. TITANIA *sleeps.*

Enter OBERON, *and squeezes the flower on* TITANIA's *eyelids.*

OBE.   What thou seest when thou dost wake,
      Do it for thy true-love take;
      Love and languish for his sake:
      Be it ounce,[6] or cat, or bear,
      Pard,[7] or boar with bristled hair,
      In thy eye that shall appear
      When thou wakest, it is thy dear:
      Wake when some vile thing is near.   [*Exit.*

Enter LYSANDER *and* HERMIA.

[4] *Newts*] small lizards.
[5] *Philomel*] nightingale.
[6] *ounce*] lynx.
[7] *Pard*] leopard.

LYS. Fair love, you faint with wandering in the wood;
   And to speak troth,[8] I have forgot our way:
  We'll rest us, Hermia, if you think it good,
   And tarry for the comfort of the day.

HER. Be it so, Lysander: find you out a bed;
  For I upon this bank will rest my head.

LYS. One turf shall serve as pillow for us both;
  One heart, one bed, two bosoms, and one troth.

HER. Nay, good Lysander; for my sake, my dear,
  Lie further off yet, do not lie so near.

LYS. O, take the sense,[9] sweet, of my innocence!
  Love takes the meaning in love's conference.
  I mean, that my heart unto yours is knit,
  So that but one heart we can make of it:
  Two bosoms interchained with an oath;
  So then two bosoms and a single troth.
  Then by your side no bed-room me deny;
  For lying so, Hermia, I do not lie.

HER. Lysander riddles very prettily:
  Now much beshrew[10] my manners and my pride,
  If Hermia meant to say Lysander lied.
  But, gentle friend, for love and courtesy
  Lie further off; in human[11] modesty,
  Such separation as may well be said
  Becomes a virtuous bachelor and a maid,
  So far be distant; and, good night, sweet friend:
  Thy love ne'er alter till thy sweet life end!

LYS. Amen, amen, to that fair prayer, say I;
  And then end life when I end loyalty!
  Here is my bed: sleep give thee all his rest!

HER. With half that wish the wisher's eyes be press'd! *[They sleep.*

Enter PUCK.

PUCK. Through the forest have I gone,
   But Athenian found I none,
   On whose eyes I might approve[12]
   This flower's force in stirring love.

---

 [8] *troth*] truth.
  [9] *take the sense*] consider the significance.
 [10] *much beshrew*] a curse on.
 [11] *human*] benevolent.
 [12] *approve*] test.

Night and silence.—Who is here?
Weeds of Athens he doth wear:
This is he, my master said,
Despised the Athenian maid;
And here the maiden, sleeping sound,
On the dank and dirty ground.
Pretty soul! she durst not lie
Near this lack-love, this kill-courtesy.
Churl, upon thy eyes I throw
All the power this charm doth owe.[13]
When thou wakest, let love forbid
Sleep his seat on thy eyelid:
So awake when I am gone;
For I must now to Oberon.   [*Exit.*

Enter DEMETRIUS *and* HELENA, *running.*

HEL. Stay, though thou kill me, sweet Demetrius.
DEM. I charge thee, hence, and do not haunt me thus.
HEL. O, wilt thou darkling[14] leave me? do not so.
DEM. Stay, on thy peril: I alone will go.   [*Exit.*
HEL. O, I am out of breath in this fond[15] chase!
      The more my prayer, the lesser is my grace.[16]
      Happy is Hermia, wheresoe'er she lies;
      For she hath blessed and attractive eyes.
      How came her eyes so bright? Not with salt tears:
      If so, my eyes are oftener wash'd than hers.
      No, no, I am as ugly as a bear;
      For beasts that meet me run away for fear:
      Therefore no marvel though Demetrius
      Do, as a monster, fly my presence thus.
      What wicked and dissembling glass[17] of mine
      Made me compare with Hermia's sphery eyne?[18]
      But who is here? Lysander! on the ground!
      Dead? or asleep? I see no blood, no wound.
      Lysander, if you live, good sir, awake.

---

[13] *owe*] possess.
[14] *darkling*] in the dark.
[15] *fond*] both doting and foolish.
[16] *my grace*] the favor I receive.
[17] *glass*] mirror.
[18] *sphery eyne*] starlike eyes.

LYS. [*Awaking*] And run through fire I will for thy sweet sake.
Transparent Helena! Nature shews art,
That through thy bosom makes me see thy heart.
Where is Demetrius? O, how fit a word
Is that vile name to perish on my sword!

HEL. Do not say so, Lysander; say not so.
What though he love your Hermia? Lord, what though?
Yet Hermia still loves you: then be content.

LYS. Content with Hermia! No; I do repent
The tedious minutes I with her have spent.
Not Hermia but Helena I love:
Who will not change a raven for a dove?
The will of man is by his reason sway'd
And reason says you are the worthier maid.
Things growing are not ripe until their season:
So I, being young, till now ripe not to reason;
And touching now the point of human skill,
Reason becomes the marshal to my will,
And leads me to your eyes; where I o'erlook
Love's stories, written in love's richest book.

HEL. Wherefore was I to this keen[19] mockery born?
When at your hands did I deserve this scorn?
Is't not enough, is't not enough, young man,
That I did never, no, nor never can,
Deserve a sweet look from Demetrius' eye,
But you must flout my insufficiency?
Good troth, you do me wrong, good sooth, you do,
In such disdainful manner me to woo.
But fare you well: perforce I must confess
I thought you lord of more true gentleness.
O, that a lady, of[20] one man refused,
Should of another therefore be abused!   [*Exit.*

LYS. She sees not Hermia. Hermia, sleep thou there:
And never mayst thou come Lysander near!
For as a surfeit of the sweetest things
The deepest loathing to the stomach brings,
Or as the heresies that men do leave
Are hated most of those they did deceive,
So thou, my surfeit and my heresy,

[19] *keen*] bitter.
[20] *of*] by.

        Of all be hated, but the most of me!
        And, all my powers, address[21] your love and might
        To honour Helen and to be her knight!   [*Exit.*

HER.   [*Awaking*] Help me, Lysander, help me! do thy best
        To pluck this crawling serpent from my breast!
        Ay me, for pity! what a dream was here!
        Lysander, look how I do quake with fear:
        Methought a serpent eat my heart away,
        And you sat smiling at his cruel prey.[22]
        Lysander! what, removed? Lysander! lord!
        What, out of hearing? gone? no sound, no word?
        Alack, where are you? speak, an if you hear:
        Speak, of all loves![23] I swoon almost with fear.
        No? then I well perceive you are not nigh:
        Either death or you I'll find immediately.   [*Exit.*

[21] *address*] direct.
[22] *prey*] act of preying.
[23] *of all loves*] in the the name of all loves.

Act III—Scene I—The wood

TITANIA LYING ASLEEP

Enter QUINCE, SNUG, BOTTOM, FLUTE, SNOUT, *and* STARVELING.

BOT.   Are we all met?

QUIN.   Pat, pat; and here's a marvellous convenient place for our rehearsal. This green plot shall be our stage, this hawthorn-brake our tiring-house;[1] and we will do it in action as we will do it before the duke.

BOT.   Peter Quince,—

QUIN.   What sayest thou, bully[2] Bottom?

BOT.   There are things in this comedy of Pyramus and Thisbe that will never please. First, Pyramus must draw a sword to kill himself; which the ladies cannot abide. How answer you that?

SNOUT.   By'r lakin,[3] a parlous[4] fear.

STAR.   I believe we must leave the killing out, when all is done.

BOT.   Not a whit: I have a device to make all well. Write me a prologue; and let the prologue seem to say, we will do no harm with our swords, and that Pyramus is not killed indeed; and, for the more better assurance, tell them that I Pyramus am not Pyramus, but Bottom the weaver: this will put them out of fear.

QUIN.   Well, we will have such a prologue; and it shall be written in eight and six.[5]

BOT.   No, make it two more; let it be written in eight and eight.

SNOUT.   Will not the ladies be afeard of the lion?

---

[1] *tiring-house*] dressing room.

[2] *bully*] good fellow.

[3] *By'r lakin*] by our ladykin (the Virgin Mary).

[4] *parlous*] perilous.

[5] *eight and six*] alternate lines of eight and six syllables, a common ballad meter.

STAR.   I fear it, I promise you.

BOT.   Masters, you ought to consider with yourselves: to bring in,—
God shield us!—a lion among ladies, is a most dreadful thing; for
there is not a more fearful[6] wild-fowl than your lion living: and we
ought to look to't.

SNOUT.   Therefore another prologue must tell he is not a lion.

BOT.   Nay, you must name his name, and half his face must be seen
through the lion's neck; and he himself must speak through, saying
thus, or to the same defect,[7]—"Ladies,"—or, "Fair ladies,—I
would wish you," —or, "I would request you,"—or, "I would
entreat you,—not to fear, not to tremble: my life for yours. If you
think I come hither as a lion, it were pity of my life: no, I am no such
thing; I am a man as other men are:" and there indeed let him name
his name, and tell them plainly, he is Snug the joiner.

QUIN.   Well, it shall be so. But there is two hard things; that is, to bring
the moonlight into a chamber; for, you know, Pyramus and Thisbe
meet by moonlight.

SNOUT.   Doth the moon shine that night we play our play?

BOT.   A calendar, a calendar! look in the almanac; find out moonshine,
find out moonshine.

QUIN.   Yes, it doth shine that night.

BOT.   Why, then may you leave a casement of the great chamber
window, where we play, open, and the moon may shine in at the
casement.

QUIN.   Ay; or else one must come in with a bush of thorns[8] and a
lantern, and say he comes to disfigure,[9] or to present,[10] the person
of moonshine. Then, there is another thing: we must have a wall in
the great chamber; for Pyramus and Thisbe, says the story, did talk
through the chink of a wall.

SNOUT.   You can never bring in a wall. What say you, Bottom?

BOT.   Some man or other must present Wall: and let him have some
plaster, or some loam, or some rough-cast[11] about him, to signify
"wall"; and let him hold his fingers thus, and through that cranny
shall Pyramus and Thisbe whisper.

QUIN.   If that may be, then all is well. Come, sit down, every mother's

---

[6] *fearful*] terrifying.

[7] *defect*] Bottom's malapropism for "effect."

[8] *bush of thorns*] The man in the moon was said to have been exiled there for collecting
firewood on Sundays.

[9] *disfigure*] Quince's malapropism for "figure."

[10] *present*] represent.

[11] *rough-cast*] plaster mixed with pebbles.

son, and rehearse your parts. Pyramus, you begin: when you have
spoken your speech, enter into that brake: and so every one
according to his cue.

Enter PUCK *behind*.

PUCK.   What hempen home-spuns[12] have we swaggering here,
        So near the cradle of the fairy queen?
        What, a play toward![13] I'll be an auditor;
        An actor too perhaps, if I see cause.
QUIN.   Speak, Pyramus. Thisbe, stand forth.
BOT.   Thisbe, the flowers of odious savours sweet,—
QUIN.   Odours, odours.
BOT.   ——odours savours sweet:
        So hath thy breath, my dearest Thisbe dear.
        But hark, a voice! stay thou but here awhile,
        And by and by I will to thee appear.   [*Exit.*
PUCK.   A stranger Pyramus than e'er play'd here.   [*Exit.*
FLU.   Must I speak now?
QUIN.   Ay, marry, must you; for you must understand he goes but to see a
noise that he heard, and is to come again.
FLU.   Most radiant Pyramus, most lily-white of hue,
        Of colour like the red rose on triumphant brier,
        Most brisky juvenal,[14] and eke most lovely Jew,[15]
        As true as truest horse, that yet would never tire,
        I'll meet thee, Pyramus, at Ninny's[16] tomb.
QUIN.   "Ninus' tomb," man: why, you must not speak that yet; that you
answer to Pyramus: you speak all your part at once, cues and all.
Pyramus enter: your cue is past; it is, "never tire."
FLU.   O,—As true as truest horse, that yet would never tire.

Re-enter PUCK, *and* BOTTOM *with an ass's head*.

BOT.   If I were fair, Thisbe, I were only thine.
QUIN.   O monstrous! O strange! we are haunted. Pray, masters! fly,
masters! Help!

        [*Exeunt* QUINCE, SNUG, FLUTE, SNOUT, *and* STARVELING.

PUCK.   I'll follow you, I'll lead you about a round,
        Through bog, through bush, through brake, through brier:

---

  [12] *hempen home-spuns*] rustics, wearing homespun clothes of hemp.
  [13] *toward*] in rehearsal.
  [14] *brisky juvenal*] nimble youth.
  [15] *Jew*] youth (a play on the first syllable of "juvenal").
  [16] *Ninny's*] Ninus, the legendary founder of Babylon.

Sometime a horse I'll be, sometime a hound,
  A hog, a headless bear, sometime a fire;
And neigh, and bark, and grunt, and roar, and burn,
Like horse, hound, hog, bear, fire, at every turn.   [*Exit.*

BOT.   Why do they run away? this is a knavery of them to make me
afeard.

Re-enter SNOUT.

SNOUT.   O Bottom, thou art changed! what do I see on thee?
BOT.   What do you see? you see an ass-head of your own, do you?
                                             [*Exit* SNOUT.

Re-enter QUINCE.

QUIN.   Bless thee, Bottom! bless thee! thou art translated.[17]   [*Exit.*
BOT.   I see their knavery: this is to make an ass of me; to fright me, if
they could. But I will not stir from this place, do what they can: I
will walk up and down here, and I will sing, that they shall hear I am
not afraid.   [*Sings.*

             The ousel[18] cock so black of hue,
                With orange-tawny bill,
             The throstle[19] with his note so true,
                The wren with little quill;[20]

TITA.   [*Awaking*] What angel wakes me from my flowery bed?
BOT.   [*Sings*]

             The finch, the sparrow, and the lark,
                The plain-song cuckoo gray,
            Whose note full many a man doth mark,
             And dares not answer nay;—

for, indeed, who would set his wit to[21] so foolish a bird? who would
give a bird the lie, though he cry "cuckoo" never so?
TITA.   I pray thee, gentle mortal, sing again:
     Mine ear is much enamour'd of thy note;
     So is mine eye enthralled to thy shape;
     And thy fair virtue's force perforce doth move me

[17] *translated*] transformed.
[18] *ousel*] blackbird.
[19] *throstle*] thrush.
[20] *quill*] musical pipe.
[21] *set his wit to*] match his wit against.

On the first view to say, to swear, I love thee.

BOT.   Methinks, mistress, you should have little reason for that: and
yet, to say the truth, reason and love keep little company together
now-a-days; the more the pity, that some honest neighbours will not
make them friends. Nay, I can gleek[22] upon occasion.

TITA.   Thou art as wise as thou art beautiful.

BOT.   Not so, neither: but if I had wit enough to get out of this wood,
I have enough to serve mine own turn.

TITA.   Out of this wood do not desire to go:
Thou shalt remain here, whether thou wilt or no.
I am a spirit of no common rate:[23]
The summer still doth tend[24] upon my state;
And I do love thee: therefore, go with me;
I'll give thee fairies to attend on thee;
And they shall fetch thee jewels from the deep,
And sing, while thou on pressed flowers dost sleep:
And I will purge thy mortal grossness so,
That thou shalt like an airy spirit go.
Peaseblossom! Cobweb! Moth! and Mustardseed!

Enter PEASEBLOSSOM, COBWEB, MOTH, *and* MUSTARDSEED.

FIRST FAI.   Ready.
SEC. FAI.   And I.
THIRD FAI.   And I.
FOURTH FAI.   And I.
ALL.   Where shall we go?
TITA.   Be kind and courteous to this gentleman;
Hop in his walks, and gambol in his eyes;
Feed him with apricocks and dewberries,
With purple grapes, green figs, and mulberries;
The honey-bags steal from the humble-bees,
And for night-tapers crop their waxen thighs,
And light them at the fiery glow-worm's eyes,
To have my love to bed and to arise;
And pluck the wings from painted butterflies,
To fan the moonbeams from his sleeping eyes:
Nod to him, elves, and do him courtesies.

FIRST FAI.   Hail, mortal!
SEC. FAI.   Hail!

22 *gleek*] joke, scoff.
23 *rate*] rank.
24 *still doth tend*] always attends.

THIRD FAI. Hail!
FOURTH FAI. Hail!
BOT.   I cry your worships mercy, heartily: I beseech your worship's
       name.
COB.   Cobweb.
BOT.   I shall desire you of more acquaintance, good Master Cobweb: if
       I cut my finger, I shall make bold with you. Your name, honest
       gentleman?
PEAS. Peaseblossom.
BOT.   I pray you, commend me to Mistress Squash, [26] your mother, and
       to Master Peascod, your father. Good Master Peaseblossom, I shall
       desire you of more acquaintance too. Your name, I beseech you, sir?
MUS.   Mustardseed.
BOT.   Good Master Mustardseed, I know your patience [27] well: that
       same cowardly, giant-like ox-beef hath devoured many a gentleman
       of your house: I promise you your kindred hath made my eyes water
       ere now. I desire your more acquaintance, good Master Mus-
       tardseed.
TITA.   Come, wait upon him; lead him to my bower.
           The moon methinks looks with a watery eye;
         And when she weeps, weeps every little flower,
             Lamenting some enforced [28] chastity.
         Tie up my love's tongue, bring him silently.   [Exeunt.

Scene II—Another part of the wood

Enter OBERON.

OBE.   I wonder if Titania be awaked;
           Then, what it was that next came in her eye,
           Which she must dote on in extremity.

Enter PUCK.

           Here comes my messenger.
                                   How now, mad spirit!
           What night-rule [1] now about this haunted grove?
PUCK. My mistress with a monster is in love.
           Near to her close and consecrated bower,

----

[26] *Squash*] unripe pea pod.
[27] *patience*] endurance in adversity.
[28] *enforced*] violated.

----

[1] *night-rule*] nighttime revelry.

While she was in her dull and sleeping hour,
A crew of patches, rude mechanicals,[2]
That work for bread upon Athenian stalls,
Were met together to rehearse a play,
Intended for great Theseus' nuptial-day.
The shallowest thick-skin of that barren sort,[3]
Who Pyramus presented, in their sport
Forsook his scene, and enter'd in a brake:
When I did him at this advantage take,
An ass's nole[4] I fixed on his head:
Anon his Thisbe must be answered,
And forth my mimic[5] comes. When they him spy,
As wild geese that the creeping fowler eye,
Or russet-pated choughs,[6] many in sort,
Rising and cawing at the gun's report,
Sever themselves and madly sweep the sky,
So, at his sight, away his fellows fly;
And, at our stamp,[7] here o'er and o'er one falls;
He murder cries, and help from Athens calls.
Their sense thus weak, lost with their fears thus strong,
Made senseless things begin to do them wrong;
For briers and thorns at their apparel snatch;
Some sleeves, some hats, from yielders all things catch.
I led them on in this distracted fear,
And left sweet Pyramus translated there:
When in that moment, so it came to pass,
Titania waked, and straightway loved an ass.

OBE.   This falls out better than I could devise.
But hast thou yet latch'd[8] the Athenian's eyes
With the love-juice, as I did bid thee do?

PUCK. I took him sleeping,—that is finish'd too,—
And the Athenian woman by his side;
That, when he waked, of force[9] she must be eyed.

Enter HERMIA *and* DEMETRIUS.

---

[2] *patches, rude mechanicals*] clowns, uncivilized workingmen.
[3] *The shallowest . . . sort*] the stupidest blockhead of that brainless company.
[4] *nole*] head.
[5] *mimic*] actor.
[6] *russet-pated choughs*] red-headed jackdaws.
[7] *at our stamp*] on hearing our footsteps.
[8] *latch'd*] moistened.
[9] *of force*] necessarily.

OBE.   Stand close: this is the same Athenian.

PUCK.   This is the woman, but not this the man.

DEM.   Oh, why rebuke you him that loves you so?
        Lay breath so bitter on your bitter foe.

HER.   Now I but chide; but I should use[10] thee worse,
        For thou, I fear, hast given me cause to curse.
        If thou hast slain Lysander in his sleep,
        Being o'er shoes in blood, plunge in the deep,
        And kill me too.
        The sun was not so true unto the day
        As he to me: would he have stolen away
        From sleeping Hermia? I'll believe as soon
        This whole earth may be bored, and that the moon
        May through the centre creep, and so displease
        Her brother's noontide with the Antipodes.
        It cannot be but thou hast murder'd him;
        So should a murderer look, so dead,[11] so grim.

DEM.   So should the murder'd look; and so should I,
        Pierced through the heart with your stern cruelty:
        Yet you, the murderer, look as bright, as clear,
        As yonder Venus in her glimmering sphere.

HER.   What's this to my Lysander? where is he?
        Ah, good Demetrius, wilt thou give him me?

DEM.   I had rather give his carcass to my hounds.

HER.   Out, dog! out, cur! thou drivest me past the bounds
        Of maiden's patience. Hast thou slain him, then?
        Henceforth be never number'd among men!
        O, once tell true, tell true, even for my sake!
        Durst thou have look'd upon him being awake,
        And hast thou kill'd him sleeping? O brave touch!
        Could not a worm,[12] an adder, do so much?
        An adder did it; for with doubler[13] tongue
        Than thine, thou serpent, never adder stung.

DEM.   You spend your passion on a misprised mood:[14]
        I am not guilty of Lysander's blood;
        Nor is he dead, for aught that I can tell.

[10] *use*] treat.
[11] *dead*] deadly.
[12] *worm*] serpent.
[13] *doubler*] more forked and more deceitful.
[14] *a misprised mood*] a fit of anger caused by a mistake.

HER.   I pray thee, tell me then that he is well.
DEM.   An if I could, what should I get therefore?
HER.   A privilege, never to see me more.
       And from thy hated presence part I so:
       See me no more, whether he be dead or no.   [*Exit.*
DEM.   There is no following her in this fierce vein:
       Here therefore for a while I will remain.
       So sorrow's heaviness doth heavier grow
       For debt that bankrupt sleep doth sorrow owe;
       Which now in some slight measure it will pay,
       If for his tender[15] here I make some stay. [*Lies down and sleeps.*
OBE.   What hast thou done? thou hast mistaken quite,
       And laid the love-juice on some true-love's sight:
       Of thy misprision must perforce ensue
       Some true love turn'd, and not a false turn'd true.
PUCK. Then fate o'er-rules, that, one man holding troth,
       A million fail, confounding oath on oath.[16]
OBE.   About the wood go swifter than the wind,
       And Helena of Athens look thou find:
       All fancy-sick[17] she is and pale of cheer,[18]
       With sighs of love, that costs the fresh blood dear:
       By some illusion see thou bring her here:
       I'll charm his eyes against[19] she do appear.
PUCK. I go, I go; look how I go,
       Swifter than arrow from the Tartar's bow.   [*Exit.*
OBE.   Flower of this purple dye,
           Hit with Cupid's archery,
           Sink in apple of his eye.
           When his love he doth espy,
           Let her shine as gloriously
           As the Venus of the sky.
           When thou wakest, if she be by,
           Beg of her for remedy.

Re-enter PUCK.

PUCK.   Captain of our fairy band,
           Helena is here at hand;

   [15] *his tender*] sleep's offering of itself.
   [16] *confounding oath on oath*] subverting one oath by another.
   [17] *fancy-sick*] lovesick.
   [18] *cheer*] countenance.
   [19] *against*] in provision for the time when.

           And the youth, mistook by me,
           Pleading for a lover's fee.
           Shall we their fond pageant[20] see?
           Lord, what fools these mortals be!
OBE.   Stand aside: the noise they make
           Will cause Demetrius to awake.
PUCK.   Then will two at once woo one;
           That must needs be sport alone;
           And those things do best please me
           That befal preposterously.[21]

Enter LYSANDER *and* HELENA.

LYS.   Why should you think that I should woo in scorn?
           Scorn and derision never come in tears:
         Look, when I vow, I weep; and vows so born,
           In their nativity all truth appears.
         How can these things in me seem scorn to you,
         Bearing the badge of faith, to prove them true?
HEL.   You do advance your cunning more and more.
           When truth kills truth, O devilish-holy fray!
         These vows are Hermia's: will you give her o'er?
           Weigh oath with oath, and you will nothing weigh:
         Your vows to her and me, put in two scales,
         Will even weigh; and both as light as tales.
LYS.   I had no judgement when to her I swore.
HEL.   Nor none, in my mind,[22] now you give her o'er.
LYS.   Demetrius loves her, and he loves not you.
DEM.   [*Awaking*] O Helen, goddess, nymph, perfect, divine!
         To what, my love, shall I compare thine eyne?
         Crystal is muddy. O, how ripe in show
         Thy lips, those kissing cherries, tempting grow!
         That pure congealed white, high Taurus'[23] snow,
         Fann'd with the eastern wind, turns to a crow
         When thou hold'st up thy hand: O, let me kiss
         This princess of pure white, this seal of bliss!
HEL.   O spite! O hell! I see you all are bent
         To set against me for your merriment:
         If you were civil and knew courtesy,

[20] *fond pageant*] foolish spectacle.
[21] *preposterously*] contrary to the natural order of things.
[22] *mind*] opinion.
[23] *Taurus'*] Taurus is a mountain range in southern Turkey.

You would not do me thus much injury.
Can you not hate me, as I know you do,
But you must join in souls to mock me too?
If you were men, as men you are in show,
You would not use a gentle lady so;
To vow, and swear, and superpraise my parts, [24]
When I am sure you hate me with your hearts.
You both are rivals, and love Hermia;
And now both rivals, to mock Helena:
A trim[25] exploit, a manly enterprise,
To conjure tears up in a poor maid's eyes
With your derision! none of noble sort
Would so offend a virgin, and extort
A poor soul's patience, all to make you sport.

LYS. You are unkind, Demetrius; be not so;
For you love Hermia; this you know I know:
And here, with all good will, with all my heart,
In Hermia's love I yield you up my part;
And yours of Helena to me bequeath,
Whom I do love, and will do till my death.

HEL. Never did mockers waste more idle breath.

DEM. Lysander, keep thy Hermia; I will none:[26]
If e'er I loved her, all that love is gone.
My heart to her but as guest-wise sojourn'd,
And now to Helen is it home return'd,
There to remain.

LYS.   Helen, it is not so.

DEM. Disparage not the faith thou dost not know,
Lest, to thy peril, thou aby[27] it dear.
Look, where thy love comes; yonder is thy dear.

Re-enter HERMIA.

HER. Dark night, that from the eye his function takes,
The ear more quick of apprehension makes;
Wherein it doth impair the seeing sense,
It pays the hearing double recompense.
Thou art not by mine eye, Lysander, found;

[24] *superpraise my parts*] overpraise my qualities.
[25] *trim*] fine.
[26] *I will none*] I want nothing to do with her.
[27] *aby*] pay for.

Mine ear, I thank it, brought me to thy sound.
But why unkindly didst thou leave me so?

LYS. Why should he stay, whom love doth press to go?

HER. What love could press Lysander from my side?

LYS. Lysander's love, that would not let him bide,
Fair Helena, who more engilds the night
Than all yon fiery oes[28] and eyes of light.
Why seek'st thou me? could not this make thee know,
The hate I bare thee made me leave thee so?

HER. You speak not as you think: it cannot be.

HEL. Lo, she is one of this confederacy!
Now I perceive they have conjoin'd all three
To fashion this false sport, in spite of[29] me.
Injurious Hermia! most ungrateful maid!
Have you conspired, have you with these contrived
To bait me with this foul derision?
Is all the counsel that we two have shared,
The sisters' vows, the hours that we have spent,
When we have chid[30] the hasty-footed time
For parting us,—O, is all forgot?
All school-days' friendship, childhood innocence?
We, Hermia, like two artificial[31] gods,
Have with our needles created both one flower,
Both on one sampler, sitting on one cushion,
Both warbling of one song, both in one key;
As if our hands, our sides, voices, and minds,
Had been incorporate.[32] So we grew together,
Like to a double cherry, seeming parted,
But yet an union in partition;
Two lovely berries moulded on one stem;
So, with two seeming bodies, but one heart;
Two of the first, like coats in heraldry,
Due but to one, and crowned with one crest.[33]
And will you rent[34] our ancient love asunder,

---

[28] *fiery oes*] circles of fire, stars.

[29] *in spite of*] out of spite for.

[30] *chid*] scolded.

[31] *artificial*] artistically creative.

[32] *incorporate*] of one body.

[33] *Two of the first, . . . crest*] Our two bodies resemble two coats of arms in heraldry, which belong to a single person, and are surrounded by a single crest.

[34] *rent*] rend, tear.

To join with men in scorning your poor friend?
It is not friendly, 't is not maidenly:
Our sex, as well as I, may chide you for it,
Though I alone do feel the injury.

HER.   I am amazed at your passionate words.
I scorn you not: it seems that you scorn me.

HEL.   Have you not set Lysander, as in scorn,
To follow me and praise my eyes and face?
And made your other love, Demetrius,
Who even but now did spurn me with his foot,
To call me goddess, nymph, divine and rare,
Precious, celestial? Wherefore speaks he this
To her he hates? and wherefore doth Lysander
Deny your love, so rich within his soul,
And tender[35] me, forsooth, affection,
But by your setting on,[36] by your consent?
What though I be not so in grace as you,
So hung upon with love, so fortunate,
But miserable most, to love unloved?
This you should pity rather than despise.

HER.   I understand not what you mean by this.

HEL.   Ay, do, persever,[37] counterfeit sad[38] looks,
Make mouths upon[39] me when I turn my back;
Wink each at other; hold the sweet jest up:
This sport, well carried, shall be chronicled.
If you have any pity, grace, or manners,
You would not make me such an argument.[40]
But fare ye well: 't is partly my own fault;
Which death or absence soon shall remedy.

LYS.   Stay, gentle Helena; hear my excuse:
My love, my life, my soul, fair Helena!

HEL.   O excellent!

HER.   Sweet, do not scorn her so.

DEM.   If she cannot entreat, I can compel.

LYS.   Thou canst compel no more than she entreat:
Thy threats have no more strength than her weak prayers.

[35] *tender*] offer.
[36] *setting on*] instigation.
[37] *persever*] persevere.
[38] *sad*] serious.
[39] *Make mouths upon*] make faces at.
[40] *make me such an argument*] ridicule me so.

       Helen, I love thee; by my life, I do:
       I swear by that which I will lose for thee,
       To prove him false that says I love thee not.
DEM.   I say I love thee more than he can do.
LYS.   If thou say so, withdraw, and prove it too.
DEM.   Quick, come!
HER.   Lysander, whereto tends all this?
LYS.   Away, you Ethiope![41]
DEM.   No, no; he'll . . .[42]
       Seem to break loose; take on as you would follow,
       But yet come not: you are a tame man, go!
LYS.   Hang off,[43] thou cat, thou burr![44] vile thing, let loose,
       Or I will shake thee from me like a serpent!
HER.   Why are you grown so rude? what change is this?
       Sweet love,—
LYS.   Thy love! out, tawny Tartar, out!
       Out, loathed medicine! hated potion, hence!
HER.   Do you not jest?
HEL.   Yes, sooth; and so do you.
LYS.   Demetrius, I will keep my word with thee.
DEM.   I would I had your bond, for I perceive
       A weak bond holds you: I'll not trust your word.
LYS.   What, should I hurt her, strike her, kill her dead?
       Although I hate her, I'll not harm her so.
HER.   What, can you do me greater harm than hate?
       Hate me! wherefore? O me! what news,[45] my love!
       Am not I Hermia? are not you Lysander?
       I am as fair now as I was erewhile.[46]
       Since night you loved me; yet since night you left me:
       Why, then you left me,—O, the gods forbid!—
       In earnest, shall I say?
LYS.   Ay, by my life;
       And never did desire to see thee more.
       Therefore be out of hope, of question, of doubt;
       Be certain, nothing truer; 't is no jest
       That I do hate thee, and love Helena.

[41] *Ethiope*] sneering allusion to Hermia's brunette complexion.
[42] *No, no; he'll . . .*] The text seems to be corrupt here.
[43] *Hang off*] let go.
[44] *burr*] the prickly envelope of the fruit on a burdock.
[45] *what news*] What is the matter?
[46] *erewhile*] up to this time.

HER.   O me! you juggler! you canker-blossom!
        You thief of love! what, have you come by night
        And stolen my love's heart from him?

HEL.   Fine, i' faith!
        Have you no modesty, no maiden shame,
        No touch of bashfulness? What, will you tear
        Impatient answers from my gentle tongue?
        Fie, fie! you counterfeit, you puppet,[47] you!

HER.   Puppet? why so? ay, that way goes the game.
        Now I perceive that she hath made compare
        Between our statures; she hath urged[48] her height;
        And with her personage, her tall personage,
        Her height, forsooth, she hath prevail'd with him.
        And are you grown so high in his esteem,
        Because I am so dwarfish and so low?
        How low am I, thou painted maypole? speak;
        How low am I? I am not yet so low
        But that my nails can reach unto thine eyes.

HEL.   I pray you, though you mock me, gentlemen,
        Let her not hurt me: I was never curst;[49]
        I have no gift at all in shrewishness;
        I am a right[50] maid for my cowardice:
        Let her not strike me. You perhaps may think,
        Because she is something lower[51] than myself,
        That I can match her.

HER.   Lower! hark, again.

HEL.   Good Hermia, do not be so bitter with me.
        I evermore did love you, Hermia,
        Did ever keep your counsels, never wrong'd you;
        Save that, in love unto Demetrius,
        I told him of your stealth[52] unto this wood.
        He follow'd you; for love I follow'd him;
        But he hath chid me hence, and threaten'd me
        To strike me, spurn me, nay, to kill me too:
        And now, so[53] you will let me quiet go,

---

[47] *puppet*] someone of short stature.
[48] *urged*] asserted.
[49] *curst*] shrewish.
[50] *right*] proper.
[51] *something lower*] somewhat shorter.
[52] *stealth*] secret flight.
[53] *so*] if.

        To Athens will I bear my folly back,
        And follow you no further: let me go:
        You see how simple and how fond[54] I am.

HER. Why, get you gone: who is't that hinders you?

HEL. A foolish heart, that I leave here behind.

HER. What, with Lysander?

HEL.   With Demetrius.

LYS. Be not afraid; she shall not harm thee, Helena.

DEM. No, sir, she shall not, though you take her part.

HEL. O, when she's angry, she is keen and shrewd!
        She was a vixen when she went to school;
        And though she be but little, she is fierce.

HER. Little again! nothing but low and little!
        Why will you suffer her to flout me thus?
        Let me come to her.

LYS.   Get you gone, you dwarf;
        You minimus,[55] of hindering knot-grass[56] made;
        You bead, you acorn.

DEM.   You are too officious
        In her behalf that scorns your services.
        Let her alone: speak not of Helena;
        Take not her part; for, if thou dost intend
        Never so little show of love to her,
        Thou shalt aby it.

LYS.   Now she holds me not;
        Now follow, if thou darest, to try whose right,
        Of thine or mine, is most in Helena.

DEM. Follow! nay, I'll go with thee, cheek by jole.[57]

                  [*Exeunt* LYSANDER *and* DEMETRIUS.

HER. You, mistress, all this coil is 'long of you:[58]
        Nay, go not back.

HEL.   I will not trust you, I,
        Nor longer stay in your curst company.
        Your hands than mine are quicker for a fray,
        My legs are longer though, to run away.   [*Exit*.

HER. I am amazed, and know not what to say.   [*Exit*.

OBE. This is thy negligence: still thou mistakest,

---

[54] *fond*] foolish.

[55] *minimus*] tiny creature.

[56] *knot-grass*] a weed that, when eaten by a child, was thought to impede growth.

[57] *cheek by jole*] cheek to cheek.

[58] *this coil is 'long of you*] this confusion is on account of you.

        Or else committ'st thy knaveries wilfully.

PUCK. Believe me, king of shadows, I mistook.
        Did not you tell me I should know the man
        By the Athenian garments he had on?
        And so far blameless proves my enterprise,
        That I have 'nointed an Athenian's eyes;
        And so far am I glad it so did sort,[59]
        As this their jangling I esteem a sport.

OBE. Thou see'st these lovers seek a place to fight:
        Hie therefore, Robin, overcast the night;
        The starry welkin[60] cover thou anon
        With drooping fog, as black as Acheron;[61]
        And lead these testy rivals so astray,
        As one come not within another's way.
        Like to Lysander sometime frame thy tongue,
        Then stir Demetrius up with bitter wrong;
        And sometime rail thou like Demetrius;
        And from each other look thou lead them thus,
        Till o'er their brows death-counterfeiting sleep
        With leaden legs and batty wings doth creep:
        Then crush this herb into Lysander's eye;
        Whose liquor hath this virtuous property,
        To take from thence all error with his might,
        And make his eyeballs roll with wonted[62] sight.
        When they next wake, all this derision
        Shall seem a dream and fruitless vision;
        And back to Athens shall the lovers wend,
        With league whose date[63] till death shall never end.
        Whiles I in this affair do thee employ,
        I'll to my queen and beg her Indian boy;
        And then I will her charmed eye release
        From monster's view, and all things shall be peace.

PUCK. My fairy lord, this must be done with haste,
        For night's swift dragons[64] cut the clouds full fast,
        And yonder shines Aurora's harbinger;[65]

[59] *sort*] turn out.
[60] *welkin*] sky.
[61] *Acheron*] a river in Hades, the water of which was black.
[62] *wonted*] normal.
[63] *date*] duration.
[64] *dragons*] the dragons drawing the chariot of night.
[65] *Aurora's harbinger*] Venus, the morning star.

       At whose approach, ghosts, wandering here and there,
       Troop home to churchyards: damned spirits all,
       That in crossways and floods have burial,[66]
       Already to their wormy beds are gone;
       For fear lest day should look their shames upon,
       They wilfully themselves exile from light,
       And must for aye consort with black-brow'd night.

OBE.   But we are spirits of another sort:
       I with the morning's love[67] have oft made sport;
       And, like a forester, the groves may tread,
       Even till the eastern gate, all fiery-red,
       Opening on Neptune with fair blessed beams,
       Turns into yellow gold his salt green streams.
       But, notwithstanding, haste; make no delay:
       We may effect this business yet ere day.   [*Exit.*

PUCK.   Up and down, up and down,
       I will lead them up and down:
       I am fear'd in field and town:
       Goblin, lead them up and down.
       Here comes one.

Re-enter LYSANDER.

LYS.   Where art thou, proud Demetrius? speak thou now.
PUCK. Here, villain; drawn[68] and ready. Where art thou?
LYS.   I will be with thee straight.[69]
PUCK.   Follow me, then,
       To plainer ground.   [*Exit* LYSANDER, *as following the voice.*

Re-enter DEMETRIUS.

DEM.   Lysander! speak again:
       Thou runaway, thou coward, art thou fled?
       Speak! In some bush? Where dost thou hide thy head?
PUCK. Thou coward, art thou bragging to the stars,
       Telling the bushes that thou look'st for wars,
       And wilt not come? Come, recreant;[70] come, thou child;
       I'll whip thee with a rod: he is defiled
       That draws a sword on thee.

---

[66] *That . . . burial*] those who have committed suicide or have drowned.
[67] *the morning's love*] Cephalus, a youthful huntsman loved by Aurora, goddess of the morning.
[68] *drawn*] sword drawn.
[69] *straight*] immediately.
[70] *recreant*] coward, deserter.

DEM.   Yea, art thou there?
PUCK. Follow my voice: we'll try no manhood here.   [*Exeunt.*

Re-enter LYSANDER.

LYS.   He goes before me and still dares me on:
       When I come where he calls, then he is gone.
       The villain is much lighter-heel'd than I:
       I follow'd fast, but faster he did fly;
       That fallen am I in dark uneven way,
       And here will rest me. [*Lies down.*] Come, thou gentle day!
       For if but once thou show me thy grey light,
       I'll find Demetrius, and revenge this spite.   [*Sleeps.*

Re-enter PUCK *and* DEMETRIUS.

PUCK. Ho, ho, ho! Coward, why comest thou not?
DEM.   Abide me, if thou darest; for well I wot[71]
       Thou runn'st before me, shifting every place,
       And darest not stand, nor look me in the face.
       Where art thou now?
PUCK.   Come hither: I am here.
DEM.   Nay, then, thou mock'st me. Thou shalt buy this dear,
       If ever I thy face by daylight see:
       Now, go thy way. Faintness constraineth me
       To measure out my length on this cold bed.
       By day's approach look to be visited.   [*Lies down and sleeps.*

Re-enter HELENA.

HEL.   O weary night, O long and tedious night,
          Abate[72] thy hours! Shine comforts from the east,
       That I may back to Athens by daylight,
          From these that my poor company detest:
       And sleep, that sometimes shuts up sorrow's eye,
       Steal me awhile from mine own company.
                                         [*Lies down and sleeps.*

PUCK.   Yet but three? Come one more;
        Two of both kinds makes up four.
        Here she comes, curst and sad:
        Cupid is a knavish lad,
        Thus to make poor females mad.

---

[71] *wot*] know.
[72] *Abate*] shorten.

Re-enter HERMIA.

HER.   Never so weary, never so in woe;
            Bedabbled with the dew, and torn with briers;
        I can no further crawl, no further go;
            My legs can keep no pace with my desires.
        Here will I rest me till the break of day.
        Heavens shield Lysander, if they mean a fray!
                                                        [*Lies down and sleeps.*

PUCK.   On the ground
                              Sleep sound:
                              I'll apply
                              To your eye,
                        Gentle lover, remedy.
                              [*Squeezing the juice on* LYSANDER's *eye.*
                              When thou wakest
                              Thou takest
                              True delight
                              In the sight
                        Of thy former lady's eye:
                        And the country proverb known,
                        That every man should take his own,
                        In your waking shall be shown:
                              Jack shall have Jill;
                              Nought shall go ill;
        The man shall have his mare again, and all shall be well. [*Exit.*

Act IV—Scene I—The same

LYSANDER, DEMETRIUS, HELENA, AND HERMIA, LYING ASLEEP

Enter TITANIA *and* BOTTOM; PEASEBLOSSOM, COBWEB, MOTH, MUSTARDSEED, *and other* Fairies *attending*; OBERON *behind unseen.*

TITA.   Come, sit thee down upon this flowery bed,
  While I thy amiable cheeks do coy, [1]
  And stick musk-roses in thy sleek smooth head,
  And kiss thy fair large ears, my gentle joy.

BOT.   Where's Peaseblossom?

PEAS.   Ready.

BOT.   Scratch my head, Peaseblossom. Where's Mounsieur Cobweb?

COB.   Ready.

BOT.   Mounsieur Cobweb, good mounsieur, get you your weapons in your hand, and kill me a red-hipped humble-bee on the top of a thistle; and, good mounsieur, bring me the honey-bag. Do not fret yourself too much in the action, mounsieur; and, good mounsieur, have a care the honey-bag break not; I would be loth to have you overflown with a honey-bag, signior. Where's Mounsieur Mustard-seed?

MUS.   Ready.

BOT.   Give me your neaf, [2] Mounsieur Mustardseed. Pray you, leave your courtesy, good mounsieur.

MUS.   What's your will?

BOT.   Nothing, good mounsieur, but to help Cavalery [3] Cobweb to scratch. I must to the barber's, mounsieur; for methinks I am

---

[1] *amiable cheeks do coy*] caress your lovely cheeks.
[2] *neaf*] fist.
[3] *Cavalery*] gentleman.

marvellous hairy about the face; and I am such a tender ass, if my
hair do but tickle me, I must scratch.

TITA. What, wilt thou hear some music, my sweet love?

Bot. I have a reasonable good ear in music. Let's have the tongs and the
bones.[4]

TITA. Or say, sweet love, what thou desirest to eat.

BOT. Truly, a peck of provender: I could munch your good dry oats.
Methinks I have a great desire to a bottle[5] of hay: good hay, sweet
hay, hath no fellow.[6]

TITA. I have a venturous fairy that shall seek
The squirrel's hoard, and fetch thee new nuts.

BOT. I had rather have a handful or two of dried peas. But, I pray you,
let none of your people stir me: I have an exposition[7] of sleep come
upon me.

TITA. Sleep thou, and I will wind thee in my arms.
Fairies, be gone, and be all ways away.[8]   [*Exeunt* Fairies.
So doth the woodbine the sweet honeysuckle
Gently entwist; the female ivy so
Enrings the barky fingers of the elm.
O, how I love thee! how I dote on thee!   [*They sleep.*

Enter PUCK.

OBE. [*Advancing*]   Welcome, good Robin. See'st thou this sweet sight?
Her dotage now I do begin to pity:
For, meeting her of late behind the wood,
Seeking sweet favours for this hateful fool,
I did upbraid her, and fall out with her;
For she his hairy temples then had rounded
With coronet of fresh and fragrant flowers;
And that same dew, which sometime on the buds
Was wont to swell, like round and orient[9] pearls,
Stood now within the pretty flowerets' eyes,
Like tears, that did their own disgrace bewail.
When I had at my pleasure taunted her,
And she in mild terms begg'd my patience,

---

[4] *the tongs and the bones*] rustic musical instruments.
[5] *bottle*] bundle.
[6] *fellow*] equal.
[7] *exposition*] Bottom's malapropism for "disposition."
[8] *be all ways away*] disperse in all directions.
[9] *orient*] from the East and, thereby, of the finest quality.

I then did ask of her her changeling child;
Which straight she gave me, and her fairy sent
To bear him to my bower in fairy land.
And now I have the boy, I will undo
This hateful imperfection of her eyes:
And, gentle Puck, take this transformed scalp
From off the head of this Athenian swain;[10]
That, he awaking when the other[11] do,
May all to Athens back again repair,
And think no more of this night's accidents
But as the fierce vexation of a dream.
But first I will release the fairy queen.

       Be as thou wast wont to be;
       See as thou wast wont to see:
       Dian's bud[12] o'er Cupid's flower[13]
       Hath such force and blessed power.

Now, my Titania; wake you, my sweet queen.

TITA. My Oberon! what visions have I seen!
    Methought I was enamour'd of an ass.

OBE. There lies your love.

TITA.   How came these things to pass?
    O, how mine eyes do loathe his visage now!

OBE. Silence awhile. Robin, take off this head.
    Titania, music call; and strike more dead
    Than common sleep of all these five the sense.

TITA. Music, ho! music, such as charmeth sleep!   [*Music, still.*

PUCK. Now, when thou wakest, with thine own fool's eyes peep.

OBE. Sound, music! Come, my queen, take hands with me,
    And rock the ground whereon these sleepers be.
    Now thou and I are new in amity,
    And will to-morrow midnight solemnly
    Dance in Duke Theseus' house triumphantly,
    And bless it to all fair prosperity:
    There shall the pairs of faithful lovers be
    Wedded, with Theseus, all in jollity.

PUCK.   Fairy king, attend, and mark:
       I do hear the morning lark.

---

[10] *swain*] peasant.
[11] *other*] others.
[12] *Dian's bud*] Agnus castus (or the chaste tree).
[13] *Cupid's flower*] the pansy.

OBE.   Then, my queen, in silence sad,[14]
        Trip we after night's shade:
        We the globe can compass soon,
        Swifter than the wandering moon.
TITA.   Come, my lord; and in our flight,
        Tell me how it came this night,
        That I sleeping here was found
        With these mortals on the ground.   [*Exeunt.*
                                            [*Horns winded within.*

Enter THESEUS, HIPPOLYTA, EGEUS, *and train.*

THE.   Go, one of you, find out the forester;
        For now our observation[15] is perform'd;
        And since we have the vaward[16] of the day,
        My love shall hear the music of my hounds.
        Uncouple in the western valley; let them go:
        Dispatch, I say, and find the forester.   [*Exit an attendant.*
        We will, fair queen, up to the mountain's top,
        And mark the musical confusion
        Of hounds and echo in conjunction.
HIP.   I was with Hercules and Cadmus once,
        When in a wood of Crete they bay'd[17] the bear
        With hounds of Sparta: never did I hear
        Such gallant chiding; for, besides the groves,
        The skies, the fountains, every region near
        Seem'd all one mutual cry: I never heard
        So musical a discord, such sweet thunder.
THE.   My hounds are bred out of the Spartan kind,
        So flew'd,[18] so sanded;[19] and their heads are hung
        With ears that sweep away the morning dew;
        Crook-knee'd, and dew-lapp'd like Thessalian bulls;
        Slow in pursuit, but match'd in mouth[20] like bells,
        Each under each.[21] A cry[22] more tuneable

---

[14] *sad*] serious, solemn.
[15] *observation*] celebration (of the rites of May Day).
[16] *vaward*] vanguard, earliest part.
[17] *bay'd*] pursued with barking dogs.
[18] *flew'd*] with large, hanging chaps.
[19] *sanded*] sandy in color.
[20] *mouth*] voice.
[21] *Each under each*] in various notes.
[22] *cry*] pack of hounds.

Was never holla'd to, nor cheer'd with horn,
In Crete, in Sparta, nor in Thessaly:
Judge when you hear. But, soft! what nymphs are these?

EGE. My lord, this is my daughter here asleep;
And this, Lysander; this Demetrius is;
This Helena, old Nedar's Helena:
I wonder of their being here together.

THE. No doubt they rose up early to observe
The rite of May; and, hearing our intent,
Came here in grace of our solemnity.[23]
But speak, Egeus; is not this the day
That Hermia should give answer of her choice?

EGE. It is, my lord.

THE. Go, bid the huntsmen wake them with their horns.

> [*Horns and shout within.* LYS., DEM., HEL., *and*
> HER., *wake and start up.*

Good morrow, friends. Saint Valentine[24] is past:
Begin these wood-birds but to couple now?

LYS. Pardon, my lord.

THE.   I pray you all, stand up.
I know you two are rival enemies:
How comes this gentle concord in the world,
That hatred is so far from jealousy,
To sleep by hate, and fear no enmity?

LYS. My lord, I shall reply amazedly,
Half sleep, half waking: but as yet, I swear,
I cannot truly say how I came here;
But, as I think,—for truly would I speak,
And now I do bethink me, so it is,—
I came with Hermia hither: our intent
Was to be gone from Athens, where[25] we might,
Without[26] the peril of the Athenian law.

EGE. Enough, enough, my lord; you have enough:
I beg the law, the law, upon his head.
They would have stolen away; they would, Demetrius,
Thereby to have defeated you and me,
You of your wife and me of my consent,
Of my consent that she should be your wife.

---

[23] *in grace of our solemnity*] in honor of our marriage.
[24] *Saint Valentine*] Birds were said to choose their mates on St. Valentine's Day.
[25] *where*] wherever.
[26] *Without*] beyond.

DEM.   My lord, fair Helen told me of their stealth,
       Of this their purpose hither to this wood;
       And I in fury hither follow'd them,
       Fair Helena in fancy[27] following me.
       But, my good lord, I wot not by what power,—
       But by some power it is,—my love to Hermia,
       Melted as the snow, seems to me now
       As the remembrance of an idle gaud,[28]
       Which in my childhood I did dote upon;
       And all the faith, the virtue of my heart,
       The object and the pleasure of mine eye,
       Is only Helena. To her, my lord,
       Was I betroth'd ere I saw Hermia:
       But, like in sickness, did I loathe this food;
       But, as in health, come to my natural taste,
       Now I do wish it, love it, long for it,
       And will for evermore be true to it.

THE.   Fair lovers, you are fortunately met:
       Of this discourse we more will hear anon.
       Egeus, I will overbear[29] your will;
       For in the temple, by and by, with us
       These couples shall eternally be knit:
       And, for the morning now is something[30] worn,
       Our purposed hunting shall be set aside.
       Away with us to Athens! three and three,
       We'll hold a feast in great solemnity.
       Come, Hippolyta.   [*Exeunt* THE., HIP., EGE., *and train.*

DEM.   These things seem small and undistinguishable,
       Like far-off mountains turned into clouds.

HER.   Methinks I see these things with parted eye,[31]
       When every thing seems double.

HEL.   So methinks:
       And I have found Demetrius like a jewel,[32]
       Mine own, and not mine own.

DEM.   Are you sure
       That we are awake? It seems to me

---

[27] *fancy*] love.
[28] *idle gaud*] useless bauble.
[29] *overbear*] overrule.
[30] *something*] somewhat.
[31] *with parted eye*] with eye out of focus.
[32] *like a jewel*] just like one who finds and possesses a jewel not his own.

      That yet we sleep, we dream. Do not you think
      The Duke was here, and bid us follow him?

HER. Yea; and my father.

HEL.   And Hippolyta.

LYS. And he did bid us follow to the temple.

DEM. Why, then, we are awake: let's follow him;
      And by[33] the way let us recount our dreams.   *[Exeunt.*

BOT. *[Awaking]* When my cue comes, call me, and I will answer: my next is, "Most fair Pyramus." Heigh-ho! Peter Quince! Flute, the bellows-mender! Snout, the tinker! Starveling! God's my life, stolen hence, and left me asleep! I have had a most rare vision. I have had a dream, past the wit of man to say what dream it was: man is but an ass, if he go about to expound this dream. Methought I was—there is no man can tell what. Methought I was,—and methought I had,—but man is but a patched[34] fool, if he will offer to say what methought I had. The eye of man hath not heard, the ear of man hath not seen, man's hand is not able to taste, his tongue to conceive, nor his heart to report, what my dream was. I will get Peter Quince to write a ballad of this dream: it shall be called Bottom's Dream, because it hath no bottom; and I will sing it in the latter end of a play, before the Duke: peradventure, to make it the more gracious, I shall sing it at her death.[35]   *[Exit.*

Scene II—Athens

QUINCE'S HOUSE

Enter QUINCE, FLUTE, SNOUT, *and* STARVELING.

QUIN. Have you sent to Bottom's house? is he come home yet?

STAR. He cannot be heard of. Out of doubt he is transported.[1]

FLU. If he come not, then the play is marred: it goes not forward, doth it?

---

[33] *by*] along.
[34] *patched*] dressed in motley.
[35] *her death*] Thisbe's death in the play.

---

[1] *transported*] carried off or transformed.

QUIN. It is not possible: you have not a man in all Athens able to
    discharge[2] Pyramus but he.
FLU.   No, he hath simply the best wit of any handicraft man in Athens.
QUIN. Yea, and the best person too; and he is a very paramour for a sweet
    voice.
FLU.   You must say "paragon": a paramour is, God bless us, a thing of
    naught.[3]

Enter SNUG.

SNUG. Masters, the Duke is coming from the temple, and there is two
    or three lords and ladies more married: if our sport had gone
    forward, we had all been made men.
FLU.   O sweet bully Bottom! Thus hath he lost sixpence a day[4] during
    his life; he could not have scaped sixpence a day: an the Duke had
    not given him sixpence a day for playing Pyramus, I'll be hanged; he
    would have deserved it: sixpence a day in Pyramus, or nothing.

Enter BOTTOM.

BOT.   Where are these lads? where are these hearts?
QUIN. Bottom! O most courageous day! O most happy hour!
BOT.   Masters, I am to discourse wonders: but ask me not what; for if I
    tell you, I am no true Athenian. I will tell you every thing, right as it
    fell out.
QUIN. Let us hear, sweet Bottom.
BOT.   Not a word of me. All that I will tell you is, that the Duke hath
    dined. Get your apparel together, good strings to your beards, new
    ribbons to your pumps;[5] meet presently at the palace; every man
    look o'er his part; for the short and the long is, our play is preferred.[6]
    In any case, let Thisbe have clean linen; and let not him that plays
    the lion pare his nails, for they shall hang out for the lion's claws.
    And, most dear actors, eat no onions nor garlic, for we are to utter
    sweet breath; and I do not doubt but to hear them say, it is a sweet
    comedy. No more words: away! go, away!   [*Exeunt.*

---

[2] *discharge*] play the part of.
[3] *a thing of naught*] something shameful, wicked.
[4] *sixpence a day*] i.e., a royal pension.
[5] *pumps*] light shoes.
[6] *preferred*] chosen for consideration.

Act V—Scene I—Athens

THE PALACE OF THESEUS

Enter THESEUS, HIPPOLYTA, PHILOSTRATE, Lords, *and* Attendants.

HIP.   'T is strange, my Theseus, that these lovers speak of.

THE.   More strange than true: I never may believe
These antique[1] fables, nor these fairy toys.[2]
Lovers and madmen have such seething brains,
Such shaping fantasies, that apprehend
More than cool reason ever comprehends.
The lunatic, the lover and the poet
Are of imagination all compact:[3]
One sees more devils than vast hell can hold,
That is, the madman: the lover, all as frantic,
Sees Helen's beauty in a brow of Egypt:[4]
The poet's eye, in a fine frenzy rolling,
Doth glance from heaven to earth, from earth to heaven;
And as imagination bodies forth
The forms of things unknown, the poet's pen
Turns them to shapes, and gives to airy nothing
A local habitation and a name.
Such tricks hath strong imagination,
That, if it would but apprehend some joy,
It comprehends some bringer of that joy;
Or in the night, imagining some fear,[5]
How easy is a bush supposed a bear!

[1] *antique*] strange.
[2] *toys*] trifles.
[3] *all compact*] entirely constituted.
[4] *Sees . . . Egypt*] sees Helen of Troy's beauty in the face of a Gypsy.
[5] *some fear*] something inducing fear.

HIP.   But all the story of the night told over,
        And all their minds transfigured so together,
        More witnesseth than fancy's images,
        And grows to something of great constancy;[6]
        But, howsoever, strange and admirable.
THE.   Here come the lovers, full of joy and mirth.

Enter LYSANDER, DEMETRIUS, HERMIA, *and* HELENA.

        Joy, gentle friends! joy and fresh days of love
        Accompany your hearts!
LYS.   More than to us
        Wait in your royal walks, your board, your bed!
THE.   Come now; what masques, what dances shall we have,
        To wear away this long age of three hours
        Between our after-supper and bed-time?
        Where is our usual manager of mirth?
        What revels are in hand? Is there no play,
        To ease the anguish of a torturing hour?
        Call Philostrate.
PHIL.   Here, mighty Theseus.
THE.   Say, what abridgement[7] have you for this evening?
        What masque? what music? How shall we beguile
        The lazy time, if not with some delight?
PHIL.   There is a brief how many sports are ripe:[8]
        Make choice of which your highness will see first.
                                    [*Giving a paper.*

THE.   [*reads*]   The battle with the Centaurs, to be sung
        By an Athenian eunuch to the harp.
        We'll none of that: that have I told my love,
        In glory of my kinsman Hercules.
        [*Reads*]   The riot of the tipsy Bacchanals,
        Tearing the Thracian singer[9] in their rage.
        That is an old device;[10] and it was play'd
        When I from Thebes came last a conqueror.
        [*Reads*]   The thrice three Muses mourning for the death
        Of Learning, late deceased in beggary.

---

   [6] *constancy*] consistency.
   [7] *abridgement*] pastime, entertainment.
   [8] *a brief . . . ripe*] a written statement of how many entertainments are ready to be
   performed.
   [9] *the Thracian singer*] Orpheus, the legendary poet.
   [10] *device*] dramatic piece.

        That is some satire, keen and critical,
        Not sorting with[11] a nuptial ceremony.
        [*Reads*]   A tedious brief scene of young Pyramus
        And his love Thisbe; very tragical mirth.
        Merry and tragical! tedious and brief!
        That is, hot ice and wondrous strange snow.
        How shall we find the concord of this discord?

PHIL. A play there is, my lord, some ten words long,
        Which is as brief as I have known a play;
        But by ten words, my lord, it is too long,
        Which makes it tedious; for in all the play
        There is not one word apt, one player fitted:
        And tragical, my noble lord, it is;
        For Pyramus therein doth kill himself.
        Which, when I saw rehearsed, I must confess,
        Made mine eyes water; but more merry tears
        The passion of loud laughter never shed.

THE. What are they that do play it?

PHIL. Hard-handed men, that work in Athens here,
        Which never labour'd in their minds till now;
        And now have toil'd their unbreathed[12] memories
        With this same play, against[13] your nuptial.

THE. And we will hear it.

PHIL.   No, my noble lord;
        It is not for you: I have heard it over,
        And it is nothing, nothing in the world;
        Unless you can find sport in their intents,
        Extremely stretch'd and conn'd with cruel pain,
        To do you service.

THE.   I will hear that play;
        For never any thing can be amiss,
        When simpleness and duty tender it.
        Go, bring them in: and take your places, ladies.
                    [*Exit* PHILOSTRATE.

HIP. I love not to see wretchedness o'ercharged,
        And duty in his service perishing.

THE. Why, gentle sweet, you shall see no such thing.

HIP. He says they can do nothing in this kind.

---

   [11] *sorting with*] befitting.
   [12] *unbreathed*] unexercised.
   [13] *against*] in expectation of.

THE.   The kinder we, to give them thanks for nothing.
        Our sport shall be to take what they mistake:
        And what poor duty cannot do, noble respect
        Takes it in might, not merit.[14]
        Where I have come, great clerks[15] have purposed
        To greet me with premeditated welcomes;
        Where I have seen them shiver and look pale,
        Make periods in the midst of sentences,
        Throttle their practised accent in their fears,
        And, in conclusion, dumbly have broke off,
        Not paying me a welcome. Trust me, sweet,
        Out of this silence yet I picked a welcome;
        And in the modesty of fearful duty
        I read as much as from the rattling tongue
        Of saucy and audacious eloquence.
        Love, therefore, and tongue-tied simplicity
        In least speak most, to my capacity.[16]

Re-enter PHILOSTRATE.

PHIL.   So please your Grace, the Prologue is address'd.[17]
THE.   Let him approach.   [*Flourish of trumpets.*

Enter QUINCE *for the* Prologue.

PRO.   If we offend, it is with our good will.
           That you should think, we come not to offend,
        But with good will. To show our simple skill,
           That is the true beginning of our end.
        Consider, then, we come but in despite.
           We do not come, as minding to content you,
        Our true intent is. All for your delight,
           We are not here. That you should here repent you,
        The actors are at hand; and, by their show,
        You shall know all, that you are like to know.[18]
THE.   This fellow doth not stand upon points.[19]
LYS.   He hath rid his prologue like a rough colt; he knows not the stop.

---

[14] *Takes . . . merit*] values it for the intention rather than for its intrinsic merit.

[15] *clerks*] scholars.

[16] *to my capacity*] as I understand it.

[17] *the Prologue is address'd*] the actor who will speak the Prologue is ready.

[18] *If . . . to know*] The mispunctuation of the Prologue reverses its intended meaning.

[19] *does not stand upon points*] (1) is not respectful; (2) does not follow the correct punctuation.

      A good moral, my lord: it is not enough to speak, but to speak true.

HIP.   Indeed he hath played on his prologue like a child on a recorder; a sound, but not in government.[20]

THE.   His speech was like a tangled chain; nothing impaired, but all disordered. Who is next?

Enter PYRAMUS *and* THISBE, WALL, MOONSHINE, *and* LION.

PRO.   Gentles, perchance you wonder at this show;
           But wonder on, till truth make all things plain.
       This man is Pyramus, if you would know;
           This beauteous lady Thisbe is certain.
       This man, with lime and rough-cast, doth present
           Wall, that vile Wall which did these lovers sunder;
       And through Wall's chink, poor souls, they are content
           To whisper. At the which let no man wonder.
       This man, with lanthorn, dog, and bush of thorn,
           Presenteth Moonshine; for, if you will know,
       By moonshine did these lovers think no scorn
           To meet at Ninus' tomb, there, there to woo.
       This grisly beast, which Lion hight[21] by name,
           The trusty Thisbe, coming first by night,
           Did scare away, or rather did affright;
       And, as she fled, her mantle she did fall,[22]
           Which Lion vile with bloody mouth did stain.
       Anon comes Pyramus, sweet youth and tall,[23]
           And finds his trusty Thisbe's mantle slain:
       Whereat, with blade, with bloody blameful blade,
           He bravely broach'd his boiling bloody breast;
       And Thisbe, tarrying in mulberry shade,
           His dagger drew, and died. For all the rest,
       Let Lion, Moonshine, Wall, and lovers twain
       At large[24] discourse, while here they do remain.

    [*Exeunt* Prologue, PYRAMUS, THISBE, LION, *and* MOONSHINE.

THE.   I wonder if the lion be to speak.
DEM.   No wonder, my lord: one lion may, when many asses do.

[20] *in government*] controlled.
[21] *hight*] is called.
[22] *did fall*] dropped.
[23] *tall*] spirited.
[24] *At large*] in detail.

WALL.   In this same interlude it doth befall
         That I, one Snout by name, present a wall;
         And such a wall, as I would have you think,
         That had in it a crannied hole or chink,
         Through which the lovers, Pyramus and Thisbe,
         Did whisper often very secretly.
         This loam, this rough-cast, and this stone, doth show
         That I am that same wall; the truth is so:
         And this the cranny is, right and sinister,[25]
         Through which the fearful lovers are to whisper.

THE.   Would you desire lime and hair to speak better?

DEM.   It is the wittiest partition that ever I heard discourse, my lord.

THE.   Pyramus draws near the wall: silence!

Re-enter PYRAMUS.

PYR.   O grim-look'd night! O night with hue so black!
             O night, which ever art when day is not!
         O night, O night! alack, alack, alack,
             I fear my Thisbe's promise is forgot!
         And thou, O wall, O sweet, O lovely wall,
             That stand'st between her father's ground and mine!
         Thou wall, O wall, O sweet and lovely wall,
             Show me thy chink, to blink through with mine eyne!
                                    [WALL *holds up his fingers.*
         Thanks, courteous wall: Jove shield thee well for this!
             But what see I? No Thisbe do I see.
         O wicked wall, through whom I see no bliss!
             Cursed be thy stones for thus deceiving me!

THE.   The wall, methinks, being sensible,[26] should curse again.

PYR.   No, in truth, sir, he should not. "Deceiving me" is Thisbe's cue:
        she is to enter now, and I am to spy her through the wall. You shall
        see, it will fall pat as I told you. Yonder she comes.

Re-enter THISBE.

THIS.   O wall, full often hast thou heard my moans,
             For parting my fair Pyramus and me!
         My cherry lips have often kiss'd thy stones,
             Thy stones with lime and hair knit up in thee.

---

[25] *sinister*] left.
[26] *sensible*] endowed with feeling.

PYR.   I see a voice: now will I to the chink,
              To spy an I can hear my Thisbe's face.
            Thisbe!
THIS.   My love thou art, my love I think.
PYR.   Think what thou wilt, I am thy lover's grace;
            And, like Limander, am I trusty still.
THIS.   And I like Helen,[27] till the Fates me kill.
PYR.   Not Shafalus to Procrus[28] was so true.
THIS.   As Shafalus to Procrus, I to you.
PYR.   O, kiss me through the hole of this vile wall!
THIS.   I kiss the wall's hole, not your lips at all.
PYR.   Wilt thou at Ninny's tomb meet me straightway?
THIS.   'Tide life, 'tide death,[29] I come without delay.
                                          [*Exeunt* PYRAMUS *and* THISBE.
WALL.   Thus have I, wall, my part discharged so;
            And, being done, thus wall away doth go.
THE.   Now is the mural down between the two neighbours.
DEM.   No remedy, my lord, when walls are so wilful to hear without
            warning.
HIP.   This is the silliest stuff that ever I heard.
THE.   The best in this kind are but shadows;[30] and the worst are no
            worse, if imagination amend them.
HIP.   It must be your imagination then, and not theirs.
THE.   If we imagine no worse of them than they of themselves, they
            may pass for excellent men. Here come two noble beasts in, a man
            and a lion.

Re-enter LION *and* MOONSHINE.

LION.   You, ladies, you, whose gentle hearts do fear
              The smallest monstrous mouse that creeps on floor,
            May now perchance both quake and tremble here,
              When lion rough in wildest rage doth roar.
            Then know that I, one Snug the joiner, am
            A lion-fell,[31] nor else no lion's dam;
            For, if I should as lion come in strife
            Into this place, 't were pity on my life.
THE.   A very gentle beast, and of a good conscience.

---

[27] *Limander … Helen*] the actors' blunders for "Leander" and "Hero," two legendary
    doomed lovers.
[28] *Shafalus to Procrus*] a blunder for Cephalus and Procris, two legendary lovers.
[29] *'Tide life, 'tide death*] whether I live or die.
[30] *shadows*] images, representations.
[31] *A lion-fell*] both a fierce lion and merely a lion's skin.

DEM.   The very best at a beast, my lord, that e'er I saw.

LYS.   This lion is a very fox for his valour.

THE.   True; and a goose for his discretion.[32]

DEM.   Not so, my lord; for his valour cannot carry his discretion; and the fox carries the goose.

THE.   His discretion, I am sure, cannot carry his valour; for the goose carries not the fox. It is well: leave it to his discretion, and let us listen to the moon.

MOON.   This lanthorn doth the horned moon present;—

DEM.   He should have worn the horns on his head.[33]

THE.   He is no crescent, and his horns are invisible within the circumference.

MOON.   This lanthorn doth the horned moon present;
              Myself the man i' the moon do seem to be.

THE.   This is the greatest error of all the rest: the man should be put into the lantern. How is it else the man i' the moon?

DEM.   He dares not come there for the candle; for, you see, it is already in snuff.[34]

HIP.   I am aweary of this moon: would he would change!

THE.   It appears, by his small light of discretion, that he is in the wane; but yet, in courtesy, in all reason, we must stay the time.

LYS.   Proceed, Moon.

MOON.   All that I have to say, is, to tell you that the lanthorn is the moon; I, the man i' the moon; this thorn-bush, my thorn-bush; and this dog, my dog.

DEM.   Why, all these should be in the lantern; for all these are in the moon. But, silence! here comes Thisbe.

Re-enter THISBE.

THIS.   This is old Ninny's tomb. Where is my love?

LION.   [*Roaring*] Oh————   [THISBE *runs off.*

DEM.   Well roared, Lion.

THE.   Well run, Thisbe.

HIP.   Well shone, Moon. Truly, the moon shines with a good grace.
                    [*The* LION *shakes* THISBE'S *mantle, and exit.*

THE.   Well moused, Lion.

DEM.   And then came Pyramus.

LYS.   And so the lion vanished.

Re-enter PYRAMUS.

---

[32] *discretion*] good sense.
[33] *horns on his head*] i.e., as the sign of a cuckold.
[34] *in snuff*] (1) needing to be snuffed; (2) offended.

PYR.   Sweet Moon, I thank thee for thy sunny beams;
                I thank thee, Moon, for shining now so bright;
            For, by thy gracious, golden, glittering gleams,
                I trust to take of truest Thisbe sight.
                    But stay, O spite!
                    But mark, poor knight,
                What dreadful dole[35] is here!
                    Eyes, do you see?
                    How can it be?
                O dainty duck! O dear!
                    Thy mantle good,
                    What, stain'd with blood!
                Approach, ye Furies fell!
                    O Fates, come, come,
                    Cut thread and thrum;[36]
                Quail,[37] crush, conclude, and quell![38]

THE.   This passion, and the death of a dear friend, would go near to
    make a man look sad.

HIP.   Beshrew my heart, but I pity the man.

PYR.   O wherefore, Nature, didst thou lions frame?[39]
                Since lion vile hath here deflower'd my dear:
            Which is—no, no—which was the fairest dame
                That lived, that loved, that liked, that look'd with cheer.[40]
                    Come, tears, confound;
                    Out, sword, and wound
                The pap[41] of Pyramus;
                    Ay, that left pap,
                    Where heart doth hop: [*Stabs himself.*
                Thus die I, thus, thus, thus.
                    Now am I dead,
                    Now am I fled;
                My soul is in the sky:
                    Tongue, lose thy light;
                    Moon, take thy flight: [*Exit* MOONSHINE.
                Now die, die, die, die, die.   [*Dies.*

DEM.   No die, but an ace,[42] for him; for he is but one.

---

  [35] *dole*] grief.
  [36] *thrum*] the tufted end of weavers' thread.
  [37] *Quail*] overpower.
  [38] *quell*] destroy.
  [39] *frame*] form, produce.
  [40] *cheer*] face.
  [41] *pap*] breast.
  [42] *No die, but an ace*] a play on die-casting terms. The "ace" is the side of a die showing
      only one spot. In Shakespearean London, "ace" was pronounced so as to be scarcely
      distinguishable from "ass" (idiot).

LYS.   Less than an ace, man; for he is dead; he is nothing.

THE.   With the help of a surgeon he might yet recover, and prove an ass.

HIP.   How chance Moonshine is gone before Thisbe comes back and finds her lover?

THE.   She will find him by starlight. Here she comes; and her passion ends the play.

Re-enter THISBE.

HIP.   Methinks she should not use a long one for such a Pyramus: I hope she will be brief.

DEM.   A mote will turn the balance, which Pyramus, which Thisbe, is the better; he for a man, God warrant us; she for a woman, God bless us.

LYS.   She hath spied him already with those sweet eyes.

DEM.   And thus she means,[43] videlicet:—

THIS.   Asleep, my love?
                        What, dead, my dove?
                    O Pyramus, arise!
                        Speak, speak. Quite dumb?
                        Dead, dead? A tomb
                    Must cover thy sweet eyes.
                        These lily lips,
                        This cherry nose,
                    These yellow cowslip cheeks,
                        Are gone, are gone:
                        Lovers, make moan:
                    His eyes were green as leeks.
                        O Sisters Three,[44]
                        Come, come to me,
                    With hands as pale as milk:
                        Lay them in gore,
                        Since you have shore[45]
                    With shears his thread of silk.[46]
                        Tongue, not a word:
                        Come, trusty sword;
                    Come, blade, my breast imbrue:[47]   [*Stabs herself.*

[43] *means*] laments.
[44] *Sisters Three*] the three beings in Greek mythology who determine human and divine fate.
[45] *shore*] shorn.
[46] *thread of silk*] the thread symbolizing his life.
[47] *imbrue*] shed the blood of.

And, farewell, friends;
Thus Thisbe ends:
Adieu, adieu, adieu.   [*Dies.*

THE.   Moonshine and Lion are left to bury the dead.

DEM.   Ay, and Wall too.

BOT.   [*Starting up*]   No, I assure you; the wall is down that parted their
fathers. Will it please you to see the epilogue, or to hear a Bergomask
dance[48] between two of our company?

THE.   No epilogue, I pray you; for your play needs no excuse. Never
excuse; for when the players are all dead, there need none to be
blamed. Marry, if he that writ it had played Pyramus and hanged
himself in Thisbe's garter, it would have been a fine tragedy: and so
it is, truly; and very notably discharged. But, come, your
Bergomask: let your epilogue alone.   [*A dance.*

The iron tongue of midnight hath told[49] twelve:
Lovers, to bed; 't is almost fairy time.
I fear we shall out-sleep the coming morn,
As much as we this night have overwatch'd.
This palpable-gross[50] play hath well beguiled
The heavy gait of night. Sweet friends, to bed.
A fortnight hold we this solemnity,
In nightly revels and new jollity.   [*Exeunt.*

Enter PUCK.

PUCK.   Now the hungry lion roars,
            And the wolf behowls the moon;
        Whilst the heavy ploughman snores,
            All with weary task fordone.[51]
        Now the wasted brands do glow,
            Whilst the screech-owl, screeching loud,
        Puts the wretch that lies in woe
            In remembrance of a shroud.
        Now it is the time of night,
            That the graves, all gaping wide,
        Every one lets forth his sprite,
            In the church-way paths to glide:

[48] *Bergomask dance*] a dance named after the Italian commune of Bergamo, noted for
the rusticity of its populace.
[49] *told*] counted.
[50] *palpable-gross*] palpably stupid.
[51] *fordone*] exhausted.

      And we fairies, that do run
         By the triple Hecate's[52] team,
      From the presence of the sun,
         Following darkness like a dream,
      Now are frolic:[53] not a mouse
      Shall disturb this hallow'd house:
      I am sent with broom before,
      To sweep the dust behind the door.

Enter OBERON *and* TITANIA *with their train.*

OBE.   Through the house give glimmering light,
         By the dead and drowsy fire:
      Every elf and fairy sprite
         Hop as light as bird from brier;
      And this ditty, after me,
      Sing, and dance it trippingly.[54]
TITA.   First, rehearse your song by rote,
      To each word a warbling note:
      Hand in hand, with fairy grace,
      Will we sing, and bless this place.   *[Song and dance.*
OBE.   Now, until the break of day,
      Through this house each fairy stray.
      To the best bride-bed will we,
      Which by us shall blessed be;
      And the issue there create[55]
      Ever shall be fortunate.
      So shall all the couples three
      Ever true in loving be;
      And the blots of Nature's hand
      Shall not in their issue stand;
      Never mole, hare lip, nor scar,
      Nor mark prodigious,[56] such as are
      Despised in nativity,
      Shall upon their children be.

[52] *triple Hecate's*] The goddess Hecate has three roles in classical mythology: as Luna in
heaven, as Diana on earth and as Proserpina in hell. Her chariot was drawn by a
"triple . . . team" of dragons.
[53] *frolic*] merry.
[54] *trippingly*] nimbly.
[55] *create*] created.
[56] *prodigious*] portentous.

With this field-dew consecrate,[57]
Every fairy take his gait;[58]
And each several[59] chamber bless,
Through this palace, with sweet peace,
Ever shall in safety rest,
And the owner of it blest.
Trip away; make no stay;
Meet me all by break of day.

[*Exeunt* OBERON, TITANIA, *and train.*

PUCK. If we shadows have offended,
Think but this, and all is mended,
That you have but slumber'd here,
While these visions did appear.
And this weak and idle theme,
No more yielding but a dream,
Gentles, do not reprehend:
If you pardon, we will mend.
And, as I am an honest Puck,
If we have unearned luck
Now to scape the serpent's tongue,[60]
We will make amends ere long;
Else the Puck a liar call:
So, good night unto you all.
Give me your hands,[61] if we be friends,
And Robin shall restore amends.

[*Exit.*

[57] *consecrate*] consecrated.
[58] *take his gait*] make his way.
[59] *several*] separate.
[60] *the serpent's tongue*] hissing (of the audience).
[61] *hands*] applause.

DOVER·THRIFT·EDITIONS

PLAYS

LIFE IS A DREAM, Pedro Calderón de la Barca. 96pp. 0-486-42124-4
H. M. S. PINAFORE, William Schwenck Gilbert. 64pp. 0-486-41114-1
THE MIKADO, William Schwenck Gilbert. 64pp. 0-486-27268-0
SHE STOOPS TO CONQUER, Oliver Goldsmith. 80pp. 0-486-26867-5
THE LOWER DEPTHS, Maxim Gorky. 80pp. 0-486-41115-X
A DOLL'S HOUSE, Henrik Ibsen. 80pp. 0-486-27062-9
GHOSTS, Henrik Ibsen. 64pp. 0-486-29852-3
HEDDA GABLER, Henrik Ibsen. 80pp. 0-486-26469-6
PEER GYNT, Henrik Ibsen. 144pp. 0-486-42686-6
THE WILD DUCK, Henrik Ibsen. 96pp. 0-486-41116-8
VOLPONE, Ben Jonson. 112pp. 0-486-28049-7
DR. FAUSTUS, Christopher Marlowe. 64pp. 0-486-28208-2
TAMBURLAINE, Christopher Marlowe. 128pp. 0-486-42125-2
THE IMAGINARY INVALID, Molière. 96pp. 0-486-43789-2
THE MISANTHROPE, Molière. 64pp. 0-486-27065-3
RIGHT YOU ARE, IF YOU THINK YOU ARE, Luigi Pirandello. 64pp. (Not available in Europe or United Kingdom.) 0-486-29576-1
SIX CHARACTERS IN SEARCH OF AN AUTHOR, Luigi Pirandello. 64pp. (Not available in Europe or United Kingdom.) 0-486-29992-9
PHÈDRE, Jean Racine. 64pp. 0-486-41927-4
HANDS AROUND, Arthur Schnitzler. 64pp. 0-486-28724-6
ANTONY AND CLEOPATRA, William Shakespeare. 128pp. 0-486-40062-X
AS YOU LIKE IT, William Shakespeare. 80pp. 0-486-40432-3
HAMLET, William Shakespeare. 128pp. 0-486-27278-8
HENRY IV, William Shakespeare. 96pp. 0-486-29584-2
JULIUS CAESAR, William Shakespeare. 80pp. 0-486-26876-4
KING LEAR, William Shakespeare. 112pp. 0-486-28058-6
LOVE'S LABOUR'S LOST, William Shakespeare. 64pp. 0-486-41929-0
MACBETH, William Shakespeare. 96pp. 0-486-27802-6
MEASURE FOR MEASURE, William Shakespeare. 96pp. 0-486-40889-2
THE MERCHANT OF VENICE, William Shakespeare. 96pp. 0-486-28492-1
A MIDSUMMER NIGHT'S DREAM, William Shakespeare. 80pp. 0-486-27067-X
MUCH ADO ABOUT NOTHING, William Shakespeare. 80pp. 0-486-28272-4
OTHELLO, William Shakespeare. 112pp. 0-486-29097-2
RICHARD III, William Shakespeare. 112pp. 0-486-28747-5
ROMEO AND JULIET, William Shakespeare. 96pp. 0-486-27557-4
THE TAMING OF THE SHREW, William Shakespeare. 96pp. 0-486-29765-9
THE TEMPEST, William Shakespeare. 96pp. 0-486-40658-X
TWELFTH NIGHT; OR, WHAT YOU WILL, William Shakespeare. 80pp. 0-486-29290-8
ARMS AND THE MAN, George Bernard Shaw. 80pp. (Not available in Europe or United Kingdom.) 0-486-26476-9
HEARTBREAK HOUSE, George Bernard Shaw. 128pp. (Not available in Europe or United Kingdom.) 0-486-29291-6
PYGMALION, George Bernard Shaw. 96pp. (Available in U.S. only.) 0-486-28222-8
THE RIVALS, Richard Brinsley Sheridan. 96pp. 0-486-40433-1
THE SCHOOL FOR SCANDAL, Richard Brinsley Sheridan. 96pp. 0-486-26687-7
ANTIGONE, Sophocles. 64pp. 0-486-27804-2
OEDIPUS AT COLONUS, Sophocles. 64pp. 0-486-40659-8
OEDIPUS REX, Sophocles. 64pp. 0-486-26877-2

DOVER·THRIFT·EDITIONS

PLAYS

ELECTRA, Sophocles. 64pp. 0-486-28482-4

MISS JULIE, August Strindberg. 64pp. 0-486-27281-8

THE PLAYBOY OF THE WESTERN WORLD AND RIDERS TO THE SEA, J. M. Synge. 80pp. 0-486-27562-0

THE DUCHESS OF MALFI, John Webster. 96pp. 0-486-40660-1

THE IMPORTANCE OF BEING EARNEST, Oscar Wilde. 64pp. 0-486-26478-5

LADY WINDERMERE'S FAN, Oscar Wilde. 64pp. 0-486-40078-6

BOXED SETS

FAVORITE JANE AUSTEN NOVELS: *Pride and Prejudice, Sense and Sensibility* and *Persuasion* (Complete and Unabridged), Jane Austen. 800pp. 0-486-29748-9

BEST WORKS OF MARK TWAIN: Four Books, Dover. 624pp. 0-486-40226-6

EIGHT GREAT GREEK TRAGEDIES: Six Books, Dover. 480pp. 0-486-40203-7

FIVE GREAT ENGLISH ROMANTIC POETS, Dover. 496pp. 0-486-27893-X

GREAT AFRICAN-AMERICAN WRITERS: Seven Books, Dover. 704pp. 0-486-29995-3

GREAT WOMEN POETS: 4 Complete Books, Dover. 256pp. (Available in U.S. only.) 0-486-28388-7

MASTERPIECES OF RUSSIAN LITERATURE: Seven Books, Dover. 880pp. 0-486-40665-2

SIX GREAT AMERICAN POETS: Poems by Poe, Dickinson, Whitman, Longfellow, Frost, and Millay, Dover. 512pp. (Available in U.S. only.) 0-486-27425-X

FAVORITE NOVELS AND STORIES: Four Complete Books, Jack London. 568pp. 0-486-42216-X

FIVE GREAT SCIENCE FICTION NOVELS, H. G. Wells. 640pp. 0-486-43978-X

FIVE GREAT PLAYS OF SHAKESPEARE, Dover. 496pp. 0-486-27892-1

TWELVE PLAYS BY SHAKESPEARE, William Shakespeare. 1,173pp. 0-486-44336-1